Tales of the River:

Journey from the Mekong Delta

by

Vinh Q. Tang

ISBN 978-1-7381921-8-2

Nghĩa Lan Nhân

Acknowledgment

The translation of the collection of Vietnamese writings by the same author has been facilitated with significant assistance from ChatGPT.

Vinh Quyen Tang
Ottawa, 02-06-2024

Preface

'Tales of the River: Journey from the Mekong Delta' is a compilation of the author's reflections spanning past and present, drawn from his various articles and books, all unified by a profound connection to the land and its people that he cherishes. This book not only delves into the thoughts and emotions of an expatriate, but also illuminates the collective pain of a populace enduring relentless upheavals amid what feels like ceaseless conflicts and wars. These tragedies have befallen the amiable inhabitants of a region blessed by nature, boasting a rich and marvelous ecosystem along the banks of the lower Mekong River and elsewhere. Within these pages, it is hoped that you will discover not only echoes of the past but also, perhaps, a concise historical narrative etched by the meandering rivers upon the S-shaped terrain along the far shores of the Pacific Ocean.

Contents

1. Tales of the River

Since ancient times, when humans settled on both banks of the river, villages and towns emerged, and a profound bond with the river formed. Initially, a natural gift, the river bestowed cool water to drink, fresh irrigation for fields, and fertile sediment to nourish the land. As time flowed onward, the river became intertwined with human history, bearing witness to and participating in tales of humor, heroism, camaraderie, and joy, yet also enduring chaotic upheavals like raging floods.

Vietnam's rivers are no exception. A 'Bạch Đằng' river of valor, a 'Hát Giang' river of fortitude, have through generations nurtured layers of silt, feeding the spirit of autonomy, the resilience to endure, and the noble sacrifices made to protect a way of life, a principle of existence, and a cultural foundation that has long been the soul of a nation. However, while rivers possess the potential to unite people, they can also serve as sources of division. These barriers may take the form of the romantic notion of lovers separated by the river's flow or as deep-seated as historical rivalries between villages on opposing banks. At times, these divisions escalate into serious conflicts, resulting in loss of life, as history has illustrated.

Nevertheless, amid these complexities, the river remains a unique gift from nature. In regions blessed by its presence, this truth is evident in myriad ways, always. It may materialize in the sight of baskets brimming with fish and shrimp, accompanied by the gentle splashes of freshly caught river treasures, as vendors transport them to market in the late afternoon. Alternatively, it might reveal itself in the excitement of pulling up a trap from the water after rainfall, as the lively sounds of fish leaping to freedom fill the air.

It could also be a catfish wriggling on a fishing hook in the moonlit night, or a voracious snakehead leaping out of the water to snatch the baited hook in broad daylight. Nature's hospitality extends further through feasts prepared by countryside folks for visiting relatives from the big city. They offer a variety of local delicacies, from grilled snakehead fish over a straw fire to freshly boiled snails from the pond, rolled up in rice paper and dipped in deliciously prepared fish sauce.

The river not only nourishes people but also benefits all living things, including plants and animals. At its delta, the river feeds into a stream that flows into a pond, a haven for insects, birds, fish, and various aquatic plants. Along its banks grow reeds, with the sound of crickets chirping in the early morning mist, frogs croaking after the rain, the whistle of a wagtail bird in the summer, or the faint chirping of sparrows every evening as they settle to sleep on the rows of paperbark trees. It's a world of purple water lilies, green water hyacinths, with yellow frogs sitting idly atop. Here, a kingfisher stands with a full belly on the edge of a fishing net pole, gazing at the sky.

Beneath the pond's surface, beside the shade of coconut trees, lies a cluster of finely smooth coontail aquatic plants or a lush green water hyacinth patch, seemingly inviting little fish to play hide and seek along the edge of its cozy white form. On the shore, a few baby dragonflies flutter delicately like strands of colorful thread in the wind, here one moment, gone the next. Or a large, sturdy dragonfly darts around, lively, flying back and forth, paying no mind to the timid golden ladybugs nestled on the water mimosa leaves, flaunting their truly charming transparent 'glass' coats.

In the homeland, the river embodies contrasting moods; it can be a tranquil haven, lazily meandering past coconut trees, or a nocturnal confidant, whispering secrets among the cork tree branches. Yet, amidst the water hyacinth clusters, adjacent to a resting sampan, behind a menacing French fort, danger lurks. A French soldier, idly fishing on his boat, may find himself ensnared by the unseen trap lurking beneath the river's surface. With a swift, merciless pull, the trap seizes its unsuspecting prey, dragging him into the abyss. Silence descends upon the river as another life succumbs to its depths, joining the countless others claimed by its murky embrace. Meanwhile, at home, an aging father sits in quiet contemplation, his gaze fixed upon the river, yearning for the return of his absent young son. Despite the calm surface, the river conceals the tragic fate of both perpetrators and victims, swallowing them whole into its unforgiving depths.

Through all the ups and downs of the fluctuating tide, from the days when a girl who rowed the boat ferrying people across the river captivated many young men in the revolution against French colonialism, to the time when she abandoned the helm for the allure of American dollars, the image of the old father waiting for his son at the dinner table in the evening still remains. Feelings may vary, but the heartfelt concerns linger. "If Heaven allows me to meet Hai again, then I'll be at peace even if I have to die," a father confided over the daily cups of rice wine, discussing his eldest son who had long joined the Northern forces. Each generation carries its own sorrows, and the pain of the next generation compounds upon that of the previous one. In this case, the father also had a second son of whom he was proud, a military officer of the Southern forces. Yet, he didn't blame his third and youngest son for buying Paris Match and other English and French magazines every month to supply to his uncle in the National Liberation Front, a proxy branch of the Northern forces, hidden in an unsuspecting villa in the heart of the city. As for the father himself, he remained a loyal civil servant since the French colonial era.

Once upon a time on the 'Cầu Ngang' bridge in a remote countryside, every day, long before sunrise, the sounds of vendors' footsteps rushing to the market mingled with innocent laughter and chatter, dissipating in the early morning mist, as if from some tranquil world. Holding torches, balancing baskets on their shoulders, the farmer's wives brought chickens, ducks, shrimp, fish, vegetables, and sweetened porridge to sell at the market. Suddenly, one day, as they reached the middle of the bridge, the vendors dropped their baskets and fled. On the bridge railing, the head of the Village Chief was found, evidently placed there overnight by someone. A few days later, on the same railing, the head of the culprit was displayed in a similar manner. From then on, every morning, people no longer heard the laughter and chatter of the vendors on the bridge, only seeing the flickering torchlights resembling phosphorous light emitting from graveyards. But with time, everything came to pass. The market had to gather, and it did. What belonged to yesterday now only remained in the memories of the river and in the imagination of a few frightened children, pointing at the dark blood stains on the bridge, teased by adults. The water under the bridge still flowed. Flowing endlessly.

Severed heads displayed on the bridge, blood staining the river, yet the river still flows - continuously flowing. Whether the ferrywoman left affectionate memories in generations of young men during wartime, or whether she departed the river to move on, it still flows endlessly. Temporary changes do not alter the millennia-long process of river formation. The harsh challenges, if just fleeting moments in a nation's history, cannot destroy the state of harmony among people. The river forgives, and people are generous.

2. Bến Hải River

At the dawn of the 20th century, Vietnam remained under the colonial grip of France. Throughout the nation, from bustling cities to remote villages, a fervent spirit of patriotism coursed through the populace, driving many to join movements aimed at securing independence from French rule. While some advocated for peaceful reforms, others chose to directly confront the colonial authorities, determined in their struggle against foreign subjugation.

Drawing inspiration from the transformative reforms under Emperor Meiji in Japan, a cadre of Vietnamese intellectuals called for similar social changes within their own country. The Russo-Japanese War of 1904 further bolstered confidence in Japan's capabilities, as news of its military triumphs reverberated across international borders and ignited the hopes of Vietnamese patriots. Reports detailing the Japanese navy's decisive victory over the Russian fleet at Lushun port, the relentless advance of Japanese forces towards Shenyang, and the subsequent occupation of Manchuria spread rapidly, captivating the imaginations of many. Initially regarded as a David-and-Goliath tale, with Japan bravely challenging the might of Russia, the steady stream of victories – both at sea and on land – gradually dispelled skepticism.

The pivotal moment came with Japan's astonishing annihilation of the entire Russian fleet in the momentous naval battle of Tsushima, a victory that resonated across continents and affirmed the reality of Japan's military prowess. For nationalist movements in Vietnam seeking alliances with Japan to break free from French colonial domination, these remarkable achievements served as a beacon of hope, reinforcing belief in the collective strength of the "yellow race." It fueled the momentum of the "Heading East" (Đông Du) Movement, which saw Vietnamese youth venturing to Japan in search of enlightenment and modernization from the land of the rising sun.

Ironically, 40 years later, the geopolitical chessboard underwent rapid transformation. With the outbreak of World War II, Japan's dominance proved catastrophic for Asia. The boots of Japanese soldiers supplanted those of the French, trampling Vietnam and sowing sorrow throughout the country. Chaos reigned supreme as people grappled with a double-edged destiny, facing both new and old adversaries.

Following the Second World War and Japan's defeat, glimmers of hope emerged beneath the Vietnamese sky. However, the dark clouds of French colonization quickly amassed strength, heralding a new phase of turmoil.

Despite the Japanese Emperor's declaration of unconditional surrender after the U.S. dropped atomic bombs, devastating Hiroshima and Nagasaki, not all Japanese forces withdrew from Vietnam. Some adhered to the Bushidō tradition, committing ritual suicide. Others, fueled by extreme nationalist fervor and skepticism regarding Japan's defeat, remained entrenched in Vietnam. They espoused the ideals of Greater East Asia and the principle of 'Asia for Asians,' embedding themselves deeply in the Vietnamese mountains to bolster the anti-French resistance.

These scattered forces, though not numerous, emerged alongside various armed factions, each vying for influence to fill the power vacuum left by the weakened French authorities and the departing Japanese army. Chaos erupted everywhere, not only due to conflicts between opposing factions but also because of deadly internal disputes within some armed groups. The situation became increasingly complicated, and it was unclear which way the country was heading.

France itself was in dire straits due to the aftermath of World War II. The colonial apparatus of France in Indochina almost completely collapsed after being controlled by the Japanese army. Therefore, the Allies had to assign the task of stabilizing the situation in Indochina to England, as the British army had extensive experience in colonial rule in Asia, from India to Malaysia and Singapore to the Malay Peninsula. Thus, the geopolitical chessboard gained another English piece.

At the corner of Saigon, a group of concerned police officers and civil servants sat around a table at their frequent coffee shop, speculating about their fates. Officer Tư voiced the concerns of his colleagues:

"I wonder if the English plan to replace the French altogether, and what they intend to do here?"

Sergeant Cừ, a notorious figure in his district, sighed with frustration,

"Well, I haven't finished learning French, so how can I possibly learn English to work for these English bosses? Or worse, what if they bring their own people to replace us?"

Teacher Hai, half-jokingly and half-seriously, tried to comfort the two policemen working for the French,

"Don't worry, gentlemen. There's nothing to fear. In this urgent situation, if the British replace you, where will they find people to help them suppress the 'rebel forces?'"

Teacher Hai was referring to the armed forces stationed in southern Vietnam that were seizing land and establishing territories all over the region. In Saigon, there was the Bình Xuyên army, and in many provinces from east to west, there were armed religious factions like the Cao Đài in Tây Ninh and the Hòa Hảo in Long Xuyên. There were also roaming gangsters, including notorious figures like Năm Chảng, who operated in the Bến Thành market area. Even within the religious factions, internal divisions were present. Although the Hòa Hảo army had General Trần Văn Soái as the overall commander, there were four generals under his command, each controlling a different area. Among them were two infamous figures known throughout the South: General Năm Lửa, based in Cái Vồn, Cần Thơ, and General Ba Cụt in Thốt Nốt, Long Xuyên, notorious for his cruelty, rumored to have driven iron nails into the ears of landlords who refused to pay him money to support his army.

Sergeant Cừ wasn't reassured and asked Teacher Hai:

"I heard that General Soái is also with the French, isn't he, Teacher?"

"Well, it's said that he has reached a joint agreement with Colonel Cluzet."

"And on the Cao Đài side, what are they planning to do?"

"I can only guess. I don't know their plans."

"I'm weary of you, Teacher. Every time I ask, you say you don't know. But, before we finish our coffee, you spill all kinds of crazy beans!"

"Well, you all know. Before the Japanese arrived, when France was still strong, some factions of the armed religious groups fought alongside the French against the Việt Minh." Teacher Hai refered to a movement of persons of various political persuasions that fought for Vietnamese independence from the French rule.

After sipping his coffee, teacher Hai continued: "When the Japanese came, they joined them against the French. In the end, when Japan lost, some sided with the Việt Minh. Everyone competes for power and benefits. Allies one day, enemies the next."

Teacher Hai shook his head, weary of the few bad apples tarnishing the reputation of venerable religions rooted in rich cultural identities, deserving of utmost respect.

A few short months after these policemen speculated about their fates, the situation in the country became clearer. England decided to wash its hands of Vietnam. While England and France may be allied countries, neighboring each other across a narrow sea strait, they have a long history of disputes and enduring conflicts. Therefore, the British government had no intention of providing long-term assistance to France in maintaining its colony. After six months of reluctantly carrying out the stabilizing mission in Indochina entrusted by the Allies, the British military quietly withdrew from Vietnam.

The colonial French government hastily reinstated itself, like a child abandoned at the market having to fend for itself. French officials once again resorted to the cunning tactics they had previously employed, creating divisions among the armed factions opposing France. They manipulated one group to eliminate another through various deceitful alliances. Additionally, they provided support to criminal gangs operating casinos, opium dens, and other notorious establishments as a means of supplementing military funding through illicit means.

Despite France's extensive efforts to maintain its colonial power in Vietnam, less than a decade later, they suffered a major and ultimately decisive defeat at the Battle of Điện Biên Phủ in May 1954.

Several weeks had elapsed since the French defeat, yet Sergeant Cừ still couldn't find peace, plagued by worry and anxiety. He wondered about his fate if France decided to withdraw from Vietnam. This morning, with a somber expression, he pedaled his bicycle to the coffee shop to gather updates about the negotiations among various parties, though he wasn't entirely certain who they were, apart from a vague understanding that influential nations were convening at the Geneva Conference in Switzerland to seek a resolution to end the Indochina War. Upon encountering Teacher Hai, before he could even exchange pleasantries, Sergeant Cừ urgently inquired:

"Do you have any news, Teacher?"

"I heard they're still in the negotiation phase."

"Do you think the French will abandon Vietnam?"

"I doubt they will. If the French wanted to wash their hands of it, they wouldn't have proposed dividing Vietnam in half to salvage the South. On paper, the South would belong to the government of the State of Vietnam, led independently by Chief of State Bảo Đại, but in reality, there are still some impositions under the French Union mechanism."

"Does Emperor Bảo Đại agree?"

"No king would want to see their country's territory divided. But it's a pity for him, in the current situation, it's like wherever the big powers decide, that's where he sits."

"How do they want to divide it, Teacher?"

"Rumor has it they're still negotiating, haggling over a few here and there."

"So, the dividing line between the two regions hasn't been settled yet?"

"No, I heard that it hasn't, but each side seems to have stated their position."

"Do you think France will compromise?"

"Even if they don't want to, they have to. France is practically bankrupt after World War II and hasn't been able to get back on its feet. Although they've received support from the US for post-war development, they've mostly used the aid money to reinforce their colonial grip everywhere from Africa to Indochina. So now, it's like France has lost all their trump cards in negotiations."

"So, we don't know how things will turn out?"

"As of today, there's talk that France's stance is to use the 18th parallel as the dividing line between the North and South. The Chinese suggest shifting the boundary slightly southward to the 16th parallel, probably aiming to take Capital Huế. They are quite something. As for the Việt Minh, it's rumored they're quietly pushing to move the boundary further south, maybe to the 13th or 14th parallel, perhaps aiming to control Đà Nẵng and Hội An as well."

Two days later, it was clear. On July 21, 1954, the Geneva Accords were declared in the city of Geneva, Switzerland, officially ending the French colonial regime in Indochina. Accordingly, the 17th parallel was designated as the temporary dividing line splitting Vietnam in half for a period of two years, before Vietnam could reunify after a general election. And, that was the beginning of the division of Vietnam after the abrupt end of French colonization. However, as history has shown, reality led to a long-term division, with two hostile governments established in two regions: the North under the government of the Democratic Republic of Vietnam and the South under the government of the Republic of Vietnam. The two authorities nominally differed only by the word 'Democratic', but in reality, there was a world of difference between the two ideologies - Communism in the North and Capitalism in the South.

In addition, the Geneva Agreement also stipulated a 10-month period from the date of Vietnam's temporary division, during which the governments in both regions were safely allowed to transfer troops from all areas to their respective territories. The people were also allowed to freely move between the two regions during the specified period. This agreement led to a mass migration, unprecedented in Vietnam's history. It was a wave of migration of millions of people from the North to the South. Conversely, tens of thousands of people who had fought against France in the ranks of the Việt Minh in the South now 'gathered' in the North.

As fate would have it, the weight of history settled upon a river - the Bến Hải River. Overnight, this unsuspecting river in the center of Vietnam, nourished by babbling streams from the majestic Trường Sơn mountain range and flowing to the Eastern Sea at the Cửa Tùng estuary, became a weapon used to cleave the country in two. The river happened to run along the man-drawn 17th parallel demarcation, dividing the nation into two halves.

3. Fleeting Calm Waters

The tumultuous years under French rule were finally over. After the painful split of the country, South Vietnam struggled to stand on its feet as a democratic nation. Rays of sunshine breaking through scattered clouds illuminated hopes and joys for many. In Saigon, the capital of South Vietnam, Mr. Năm, a former police officer under French colonial rule, continued his job with the new South Vietnamese government.

He greatly valued the "radio cabinet" he bought cheaply from a French soldier married to a Vietnamese woman, before the couple and their young son had to leave Vietnam after the ceasefire agreement in Indochina was declared in Geneva on July 21, 1954. Mr. Năm called it a "radio cabinet" because the radio was placed on a high-quality yellow varnish cabinet used to store record players and records underneath. For over a decade, it sat in the living room, under the pendulum clock, to keep him company. Mrs. Năm would often complain, "He just sits there hugging that radio all day."

And holding on to it inseparably, he did. Every time there was political turmoil or a military coup in the country, Mr. Năm would sit for hours in front of the radio cabinet, eagerly listening to the news. Sometimes he seemed anxious, restless, unable to sit still; other times he appeared melancholic. Occasionally, he would suddenly stand up, embrace the radio cabinet, and start dancing with it, perhaps partly due to the influence of wandering spirits - the rice wine he consumed often. Once, in one of those moments, Mrs. Năm walked by, minding her own business with floor sweeping, and Mr. Năm grabbed her to serve as his dancing partner. She blushed and withdrew from his embrace, teasingly saying, "What's gotten into you today?," before shyly retreating into the back of the house. Their eldest daughter, Thanh, worried that her father might get arrested, even though he had served as a police officer under two regimes, first under the French and then under the Republic of Vietnam. But with the frequent changes in power, she thought one never knew what might happen.

Moreover, recently, Teacher Hai's daughter followed her mother's instructions to inform her father's drinking buddies, including Mr. Năm, that her father had been arrested by the police. Mr. Năm hastily took out all the newspapers and books stored in the old ancestral altar and threw them into a barrel near the chicken coop behind the house to burn, simply because among them there may be some books and articles he received from Teacher Hai, and now he couldn't distinguish one from another. Later, Mr. Năm's eldest son, Bình, found himself sitting with tears streaming down his face because he had lost all the precious books and magazines that he had carefully preserved for many years. Every time this incident was mentioned, he felt heartaches, especially for the series "The Skull-and-Crossbones Bandit". He particularly liked the way they broadcast their messages, through lines of text projected onto the sky of Saigon above the Bến Thành Market using laser beams. At such times, traffic would stop, and everyone would crane their necks to anxiously follow the announcements of instant justice against evil and tyranny!

For the past few years, every week Mr. Năm has tuned in to the lottery program, to listen to the National Lottery Song by "Bizarre Talent" Trần Văn Trạch on his radio. Whenever Mr. Năm feels excited, he turns up the volume, and the more excited he gets, the louder he turns it up to share his joy with the neighborhood. The beloved song could be understood as:

"National lottery
Aiding our fellow citizens
Constructing countless futures
Where owning homes is within reach.

...

Fortunes await, just five or ten bucks away
A chance to secure a home and a car
Wealth bestowed overnight..."

Mr. Năm was even more fascinated by Mr. Trần Văn Trạch's 'comedy talent,' especially upon hearing his performance of the song 'The Train Journey on the 5th Day of Tết (Vietnamese New Year) Celebration.' This song depicted a scene of a passenger on a long-distance train, passing time by counting the lampposts flashing past outside the window. The narrative unfolded with the passenger encountering another traveler, engaging in a series of questions, all while Mr. Trạch adeptly juggled both answering and counting lampposts simultaneously. The resulting conversation was a delightful mix of humor and spontaneity, leaving Mr. Năm stroking his beard in sheer delight.

Additionally, Mr. Trạch skillfully transported the listeners to the train station by vividly imitating the sounds of the engine revving up, the whistle blowing, and the subsequent clattering of the train as it started to roll along the tracks. Even as several cars gained full speed, the noise of the train bustling along the railroad continued. Alone in front of his radio, Mr. Năm couldn't contain his laughter, thoroughly enjoying the performance.

Mr. Năm is also a soccer enthusiast and never misses an opportunity to listen to sports columnist Huyền Vũ narrate matches from Cộng Hòa Stadium or Tao Đàn Stadium. His commentary style is lively and captivating. Mr. Năm even turns up the volume of his radio so the whole neighborhood can listen together. "Listening alone isn't fun," he says.

The audience is enthralled as they follow Huyền Vũ's narration, listening intently as he recounts each kick of the ball, each pass, whether fast or slow, all of which they can 'see' through his unique wording and storytelling style. Huyền Vũ keeps his listeners on the edge of their seats with his often suggestive descriptions, such as when a player enters 'deep into the forbidden area,' sometimes from the right wing, sometimes from the left. He surprises them with 'lightning-fast shots' that occasionally 'shatter the goal frame,' but more often than not, he describes balls 'skipping past defenders' amidst the collective gasps and exclamations of his audience. After several minutes of back-and-forth play without a goal, Huyền Vũ kindly reassures his listeners: 'Both sides' nets are still virgin.'

Another talent of Huyền Vũ that fans often mention is his remarkable ability to remember the names of foreign players, from places like Indonesia, Malaysia, or Thailand, with their lengthy, exotic names, which he recites effortlessly, without ever stumbling.

Mr. Năm is in his senior years. Typically, as one grows older, the anticipation for Tết diminishes, and the allure of Tết isn't as strong as it once was. Fortunately for Mr. Năm, in recent years, he had rediscovered a sense of excitement in his heart while awaiting Tết. He found the yellow apricot blossom on the ancestral altar more cheerful, and the drumming sound accompanying the lion dance together with the explosions of firecrackers more enjoyable. All this was thanks to the emergence of the AVT musical band. A great pleasure for Mr. Năm in recent Tết seasons was tuning in to the AVT radio show, listening to witty, satirical songs performed in three different accents - Northern, Central, and Southern - engaging in sharp, humorous exchanges.

Even the most discerning listeners couldn't resist bursting into laughter, becoming addicted to listening again and again, to lyrics like these:

"Quietly listening to them wishing each other (uh uh)
Wishing each other strength and health like buffaloes
Wishing each other wealth as abundant as water (oh oh oh)
Wishing just gave birth... then expecting... expecting again..."

The entire family enjoys listening to the AVT band, not just Mr. Năm. However, his daughter sometimes shows unease or shyness towards lyrics that might touch the hearts of young girls entering adolescence, or phrases that tease the sexual prowess of older men. As for Mrs. Năm, there is no modern music program that she enjoys other than the AVT band's. However, she also comments, "The guy from the North and the Việt guy sound fun, but I really can't understand what the guy from the Central region is saying." Mr. Năm responds curtly, "I've told you repeatedly, whether from the North, Central, or South, we are all Vietnamese. If we live in the South, then we are Southern people, not any Việt guy.

Beside a few of his favorite programs, Mr. Năm doesn't like listening to anything else on his beloved radio. He criticizes modern music, saying the singer's name sounds like a racehorse's name, even though the two matters are totally unrelated. That's why Mrs. Năm keeps scolding him, "You're too old-fashioned." He also criticizes traditional Viet opera or nostalgic songs as too sentimental. As for the Tao Đàn Poetry Recitation Program by the infamous Đinh Hùng, featuring the unique and melodious sound of the 'magic flute' by Nguyễn Đình Nghĩa, only his daughter Thanh is passionate about. Every week, she eagerly waits for Saturday night to listen. Thanh even bought a small Japanese transistor radio for herself to comfortably listen to singer Hoàng Oanh's poetry recitations, without anyone disturbing her.

Mrs. Năm is deeply enamored with Cải lương (Vietnamese reformed opera). Each day, she eagerly awaits the passage of the advertising carriage in front of her house, just to catch a glimpse of the evening's featured play. This carriage, originally used for transporting fish to the market in the morning, transforms by midday into a spectacle, adorned with a massive lion dance drum at its center. A spirited individual energetically beats the drum as the carriage traverses the neighborhood, heralding the upcoming performance with banners on either side, showcasing larger-than-life images of glamorous actors and actresses. Lately, Mrs. Năm has developed a particular fondness for a young actress named Hương Lan, the daughter of the renowned classical singer, Hữu Phước. Mrs. Năm often marvels, saying, "Hữu Phước's little girl is only 5 years old but she's so good, you guys!"

As for Bình, he prefers modern music, but his choice of music is always criticized by his friends as "old-fashioned," with some even adding an extra word to become "old-fashioned and dull." This is because whenever he feels inspired, he just sings a few songs that he learned from the playground of Lý Thái Tổ Elementary School, with the physical education teacher whom they called "Coach". The "Coach" stands in the middle of the playground wearing a whistle dangling from his chest, counting, "One, two, three, four" ... "One, two, three..." ..."One, two... One, two." The students run around the field loudly singing:

"Here flows the Bạch Đằng River, majestic and brave,
The lineage of the Fairy Dragon,
The Lạc Hồng race, the heroes of the North and South...
... The white water flows under the vast sky.
Since ancient times, it has raised the banner of heroes,
Despite thunder, lightning, and rain or shine,
Bạch Đằng still shines to illuminate the common lineage."

As you sing, you feel goosebumps grow. That's the song of the Bạch Đằng River. Another song is 'Strong for the Nation'.

Strong for the nation, rebuilding the country.
Our youth contribute their talents.
Improving people's livelihood to rival others in the world.
Uniting to build prosperity for the southern nation.
Strong for the nation, with steadfast determination.
The Lạc Hồng race, mighty and boundless.
In adversity, we are courageous; life and death mean little.
Vietnamese youth, brave for eternity.

Bình cannot avoid teasing; society is peaceful now. It's the time of 'hundred flowers blossoming', welcoming new opportunities. People have entered the era of 'The sky is pink, shining brightly', of 'Every year as summer arrives, there's a subtle sadness', of 'On Spring days, we lift our cups in well-wishes everywhere', or of 'Today is tranquil, the wind gently sways the branches, caressing the hem of the long dress...' With many songs becoming an indispensable part of the musical festivities at year-end parties, school reunions, or traditional wedding ceremonies.

4. Saltwater Canal

In peacetime, even if it was just the calm before a storm, many people who had previously sought refuge in the big cities now felt sufficiently safe to return to their ancestral lands, either for visits or to resume their lives.

Minh felt a knot of anxiety tighten in his stomach at the thought of seeing Thành again. It had been nearly two years since they parted ways at the end of their third-grade summer at elementary school. Besides being the same age, they had grown up as close as brothers, living in neighboring houses on the outskirts of Saigon with only a pond between them.

Their bond was deep-rooted, forged from years of shared laughter and youth adventures. However, three years ago, Thanh's grandfather passed away in Long Hựu, a village nestled along the Saltwater Canal region beside the Vàm Cỏ River. This event led Thanh's family to return to their ancestral home, leaving behind the hustle and bustle of the city. Thanh's father, driven by a sense of duty, assumed responsibility for maintaining their family's land and honoring their ancestors through annual rituals.

Meanwhile, Thanh's brother, Công, remained in Saigon to pursue his studies. Today, marked a special occasion as Công was visiting his homeland, and Minh's mother had granted Minh permission to accompany him on this journey to reunite with Thanh. Sitting beside Công in the car, Minh found himself lost in his own thoughts as they traveled southward. The familiar sights passed by as they drove - the Ông Thìn bridge, the bumpy, muddy roads with their countless potholes. These sights had become almost second nature to Công through his frequent visits over the past two years.

Breaking the silence, Công turned to Minh and initiated a conversation, his voice cutting through the tension in the air. "Remember those days when you and Thanh would play together non-stop?"

Công deliberately evokes childhood memories between Minh and Thành. Minh smiles and replies,

- Yes.

- I remember, every day after breakfast, Thành would disappear. My mom said he went over to your house to play.

- Yes.

Công leans against Thành's shoulder,

- So tell me, what did you two do outside all day?

- Oh, a little bit of everything.

Công tries harder to spark a conversation,

- Well, tell me about one thing then.

Minh responds without hesitation,

- Well, we used to catch dragonflies.

- And what's so fun about that?

Minh lowers his head, smiling shyly, recounting the times they chased each other because of teasing while catching dragonflies. Whenever one saw the other quietly approaching to grab a dragonfly's tail, they would sneak up behind and disrupt the scene by suddenly shouting:

'Dragonflies have wings to fly,
Two little ones reaching out to catch you.'

Just that excuse was enough for them to chase each other, laughing, embracing each other on the grass for a while. When they returned home, their clothes were dirty, sometimes they even got scolded.

Poor dragonflies, they've always been content to serve as weather indicators for farmers:

'Dragonfly, Dragonfly, flying low means rain is near,
Flying high means it's sunny; it's time to crack a coconut to feed the
lover.'

But if they were unfortunate enough to fall into Thành and Minh's sights, it was tough luck for them. The various-sized dragonflies fluttered around the pond behind Minh's house, often harassed by the two. Perhaps only the tiny dragonflies, delicate as thread, with their transparent wings, were spared. They were elusive, appearing and disappearing under the glaring sun, difficult to spot and catch. The tiny dragonflies often flew back and forth, rarely settling in one place for the two troublemakers to disturb.

Dragonflies come in various sizes. The truly large ones are like buffalo dragonflies, their bodies adorned with green and black stripes like those of African zebras. Their heads are equipped with a pair of large, protruding eyes, resembling the headlights of a car, always darting around, watching mischievous kids like Minh and Thành. Most other dragonflies are half the size but come in more eye-catching colors. Some are radiant red, some vibrant yellow, and a few are deep blue. When they perch somewhere, on a blade of grass or a water lily leaf, they always extend their long, transparent wings gracefully. No wonder the Japanese people consider them symbols of strength and happiness.

Children like to catch dragonflies to observe, satisfying their curiosity, and then release them. However, there are also some naive ones who believe the foolish urging of mischievous older siblings, allowing dragonflies to bite their navels supposedly to teach them how to swim. Minh and Thành did not fall for the trick, not because they're more cunning than anyone else, but because since they were young, the top concern of adults in both families was that they might slip and fall into the ponds around the house. Therefore, they were taught to swim at a very early age.

The pond behind Minh's house is vast and expansive, connecting to the Kinh Dôi canal, which the French dug in the past to facilitate water transportation from the Saigon River to Bến Lức through two branches: Kinh Tẻ and Rạch Bến Nghé. Thanks to this, the pond has fresh water flowing in every day, nourishing many plants along the banks and aquatic life below.

On the surface of the pond, at times there are patches of green wolffia aquatic plants, while at other times there are floating water lilies, creating a haven for plump, white ducks owned by Mr. Tư in the nearby village. Whenever he entices them into the pond, the cacophony of quacks abruptly ceases as they eagerly consume the fresh wolffia, moving from right to left until it's all gone. During the season of large water lilies, Mr. Tư rows out to collect them for pig feed, and he also snags a few golden frogs lurking for prey on the green lily pads, using them as bait to catch some pond fish.

The bus continued to rumble and jolt, sometimes moving, sometimes stopping to pick up passengers. Approaching Cần Đước market, Mr. Công turned to Minh again and asked,

- Anything else fun to share with me?

- Well, we also often go fish scooping.

- Where do you scoop?

- Well, usually by the pond behind our house.

Minh then had the chance to share with Mr. Công the clandestine activity of scooping up colorful gourami fish that he and his friend Thanh believed only they knew about. Along the banks of the pond behind Minh's house, a row of coconut trees leaned over the water's surface, casting a sparse shadow of coconut leaves, enough to shelter the natural ornamental fish, sparkling green and shimmering purple, lurking among the roots woven into bundles resembling spread-out chopsticks. Whenever the two friends stumbled upon a cluster of white foam floating on the water's surface, signaling a fish nest, they took turns waiting nearby to catch sight of any beautiful fish wandering around their sanctuary.

Seeking out a favored, shimmering gourami fish, nestled beneath a cluster of white foam, one of the two friends would cautiously approach, one hand holding a basket, the other gripping onto a coconut tree trunk, leaning out over the pond, scooping up the entire fish nest into the basket. Sometimes they would catch fish, sometimes not. Success or failure was just a matter of luck, but what was truly regrettable were those times when they had seen the fish in the basket, yet... with a flick of its tail, it would dart out of the basket; with a splash, it would touch the water's surface, disappearing into the lush, smooth, silky green coontail aquatic plants, leaving behind two pairs of eyes staring at each other in lament.

Just as Minh finished recounting the tale of catching gurami fish for Mr. Công, the bus slowly inched its way to the final destination, halting on the empty land beside the Kinh Nước Mặn ferry dock. Adjacent to it stood a low-roofed leaf hut, with two weathered wooden tables arranged on the ground in front of the yard. A handful of men with sparse beards sat on stools, leisurely sipping tea, their eyes fixed with curiosity on each passenger disembarking from the bus. Minh followed Công onto the ferry. They opted to walk back to his family's house instead of taking the horse carriage, to save on the fare, Công remarked. The sun beat down relentlessly, the dry fields bore deep cracks. "Indeed, signs of saline soil, making it challenging to cultivate anything," Minh pondered. As he ambled and surveyed his surroundings, Minh furrowed his brows in surprise, noting the scarcity of familiar trees from his hometown Long Xuyên in the more fertile region of the Mekong Delta.

Minh recalled the time he spent on the ferry crossing the river. Though he caught glimpses of the familiar coconut palm clusters on the opposite shore, the absence of water hyacinths floating on the river struck him. Instead, he encountered only the relentless rush of the current, with waves far higher than those he was accustomed to in his hometown's rivers, crashing against the boat's sides.

As he walked, Minh couldn't help but notice the lack of fig trees and white mangroves providing shade along the dirt roads, nor the tempting passionfruit vines offering sweet refreshment. The only respite came from the ample breeze, moderating the sun's harsh rays.

Despite the tranquil rural scenery, Minh felt a subtle unease gnawing at him. A feeling intensified when he sensed a buffalo in a nearby field fixating on him. As Công astutely observed, 'Buffaloes are used to seeing farmers in their traditional black pajamas,' so Minh's white shirt might be unsettling them.

From afar, Công pointed out to Minh the direction of his family's house, located behind the tamarind tree on the right side of the dirt road leading to Saltwater Canal market. Approaching the house, Thành and Út, Thành's younger sibling, rushed out onto the road to greet Công. The two children were surprised but equally delighted to see Minh again. The classical three-section house stood behind a row of towering black wooden pillars. Elevated on a high foundation, access to the house required climbing two cement steps.

Mr. and Mrs. Tám, Thành's parents, joyfully greeted their son Công, inquiring about everything. Mr. Tám then turned to Minh and asked, "Are your parents doing well?" Minh replied softly, "Yes," and Mr. Tám continued, "I guess the 'Cách' tree by your house's sidewalk is still there, right?" Minh was momentarily surprised, not understanding Mr. Tám's intention, although he immediately thought of the tree planted by his father next to the ditch beside his house.

Mr. Tám muttered, "Your poor father, every time he has some good drinking snacks, he always calls me over to have a drink with him. At noon, if I hear him shout, 'Mr. Tám, are you there?' I know it's time to drink. Most of the time it's not much, he just picks a few leaves from the 'Cách' tree, wraps small chunks of beef in them, then puts them on the grill. That's enough for the two of us to enjoy half a small bottle of rice wine."

Mrs. Tám picked up from there, "Mentioning the 'Cách' tree reminded me that next to the guava tree at his house, there's also a vegetable garden that I'm envious of. They have all kinds of vegetables, a whole variety. His mom always insists, whenever we need some herbs like coriander or basil, just come over and pick them. Sometimes I even ask for a bunch of watercress to make salad."

Mrs. Tám also remembered something else and recounted it with much appreciation: "In the corner of the garden, there's also a bunch of pennywort growing abundantly. Back when the kids were still small, every time one of them had a fever, I'd go over there to pick a basket of pennywort and then squeeze out the juice for them to drink."

After lunch, Thành led Minh out to the back of the house to play. With just a few steps, Minh found himself amazed at every turn. Although Minh returned to his hometown in the upper region of the Mekong Delta every year for his grandfather's death anniversary, he couldn't help but be astonished by the sight of the fields behind Thành's house. Stepping out of the line of large earthenware jars holding rainwater along the side of the house, the sight of clusters of mangrove roots emerging from the muddy fields caught Minh's attention. Minh exclaimed,

- Are those mangrove trees?

Minh curiously approached a mangrove tree nearby to observe. Suddenly, there was a sudden rustling noise, xuệch ... xuệch, making Minh startle and step back.

Thành explained,

- Those are mudskippers.

Minh widened his eyes to observe. Indeed, there were two or three tube-shaped fish, jet-black, large as a child's forearm, each with a pair of protruding eyes on the top of their heads, lying motionless on the mudflat. Minh suddenly felt as if there were also some fish on the upper parts of the roots which are totally exposed to air. He stared intently. He couldn't believe his eyes. Minh stepped closer. Xuęch ... xuęch, it was unbelievable, but Minh seemed to see those creatures darting swiftly along a stretch of the tree trunk before plunging into the mud and 'running' further on the mud surface to evade detection. Minh excitedly recounted to his friend, who calmly replied, "Yeah, they keep climbing up the tree!" It turns out that they could use their two front fins as legs to 'run' on muddy ground or 'climb' up tree trunks. Minh was amazed by this discovery.

Behind Thanh's house was a low-lying area where water flowed in and out with the tides. Now that the water was receding, Minh scanned the muddy area behind the house and suddenly exclaimed, "There's a crab!" Thành chuckled, "That's a horn-eyed ghost crab. People also call them wind crabs because they can move so fast, like the wind. They're different from the crabs we've seen around our house before."

A few crabs cautiously peeked out of the cave mouths, their movements quick and fleeting as they darted from one hiding spot to another amidst the multitude of holes dotting the muddy surface. Minh, brimming with excitement, recited a folk verse:

"The wind carries, the wind pushes, let's journey to the cultivated land for wind-crabs,
To the river for fish, to the fields for crabs."

Observing Minh's delight, Thành inquired, "Interested in crab-catching, are we? We can embark on that adventure tomorrow. Today, let's indulge in the thrill of goby fish catching instead."

Minh was intrigued, responding with a quick 'yes' in acknowledgment, and followed Thành to the Saltwater Canal market. Passing by the tailor shop, the pharmacy, the hair salon, they arrived at the horse carriage station. Thành wandered around the station, eyes fixed on the ground. Minh curiously asked,

- What are you looking for?

- Horse hair.

- Why?

After picking up a strand of horse tail hair, Thành explained, "We'll fashion a loop to catch fish." Minh quickly understood and joined Thành in gathering a few long and sturdy strands. Back at home, Thành utilized two bamboo branches as fishing rods, and the strands of horse hair as fishing lines. At the end of each line, a loop was meticulously made in a noose-like fashion. No hooks were necessary; one simply stood by the edge of the field, lowered the loop into the water, attempted to ensnare a passing fish, and swiftly yanked it up.

There was no shortage of fish swimming around. As the water level rose just above the muddy surface, many little fish could be observed darting back and forth in search of food. However, this method of fishing relied heavily on luck. While one could successfully snare a fish and lift it out of the water, it often managed to slip out of the noose and return to the water. With a stroke of fortune, the friends occasionally managed to bring a fish onto the ground, only for it to squirm its way back into the water before they could laid their hands on it.

Nevertheless, Thành felt that these fleeting successes were enough to evoke fond memories of their adventurous experiences as neighbors on the outskirts of Saigon.

Never had Minh witnessed such a straightforward method of fishing, even without a hook and bait. Perhaps except for last summer, during Minh's visit to the countryside in An Giang, where he unexpectedly joined his uncle, Uncle Nine, in a fishing activity. Not far away, it occurred right at the doorstep of Uncle Nine's house. That morning, they stood on the front porch, gazing down at the glimmering pool of water in the front yard. It's a common scene in the region during the flood season. That's why people in the area, if poor, build houses on stilts, and if wealthy, build houses on high foundations, like Uncle Nine's house. If villagers need to move around, they have to use their boats, often moored right next to their houses.

Suddenly, Uncle Nine pointed down to the water in the front yard and said,

- Look, Minh, there are fishes swimming around.

The first time Minh saw fish swimming in the front yard, with a few of them even venturing near under his feet, he was excited, pointing them out to his uncle Nine. "Here's a catfish, there's a carp." Seeing Minh so fascinated, Uncle Nine asked, "Do you want to fish?"

Minh quickly nodded. Uncle Nine disappeared into the back of the house and emerged with a meter-long bamboo fishing rod, slender as his thumb. Minh eagerly accepted it, running his fingers over each smooth, golden section of bamboo. "Must be brand new," he surmised, noting the pristine condition of the white fishing line. However, a crucial element was missing: bait. "For catfish, worms are the way to go," Minh thought, but he was stumped as to where to find them in the waterlogged surroundings.

As Minh pondered, he watched Uncle Nine place a chair on the divan, climb up, and deftly pluck a piece of spider's nest from the roof beam. Rolling it between his fingers, Uncle Nine approached, defying Minh's expectations by using the spider's nest as bait. With the fishing preparations complete, Minh stationed himself at the doorstep, dropping the unconventional bait into the water-filled yard and patiently waiting for a bite.

By noon, as the waters receded, a satisfying sight greeted them: two grilled catfish, expertly marinated in ginger fish sauce, adorned the family dining table.

Thành noticed that Minh's interest in loop fishing was waning, so he invited him to the front yard to play 'đáo' - a traditional Vietnamese game where two or more children throw a bunch of coins onto the ground in front of them, taking turns throwing a stone to hit a designated coin. It was their favorite game when they were young. As they played, Minh kept stealing glances at the dangling mangoes on the branches. Thành could read his friend's thoughts and said, "Those mangoes are sour, not good to eat." Minh asked, "Why didn't they plant sweet mangoes?" Thành explained, "This tree was planted by my grandfather long ago. But according to my dad, the water in this area has been heavily salinized, so only sour mangoes grow here."

The 'đáo' game, a nostalgic reenactment of their childhood pastime, seemed less appealing now that they had both grown older. Minh looked around absentmindedly once more and then asked, "Do you remember the guava and plum trees in front of your old house?"

Thành's voice carried a tinge of nostalgia as he reminisced, "Yeah, those guavas were something else, as big as oranges. Even the sour ones tasted sweet." Minh chuckled, a hint of mystery in his voice, as he posed a question, "Can you recall what else inhabited the guava tree in front of your house?" "Just fruits, nothing more," Thành replied. Then, a sudden recollection crossed his mind, "Or perhaps you're referring to the paper bags my dad used to shield the ripe fruits from bats." Minh nodded knowingly, "Ah yes, now that you mention it, I remember those too. The gray paper bags hanging from the branches were a familiar sight. But what I meant were the ant nests." Thành smiled, understanding his friend's intent, "You're talking about the times when my brother Công used to poke those golden ant nests, aren't you?"

Growing up together since childhood, they shared a treasure trove of memories. Even now, such tales held them captivated. Golden ants often constructed their nests using leaves on the guava tree in front of Thành's house. Whenever Công fancied fishing, he'd prod the ant nest to gather ant eggs as bait. His makeshift ant-poking tool consisted of a basket crafted from mosquito-net mesh suspended at the end of a tall bamboo pole. Standing beneath the tree, he'd nudge the nest with the pole until it dropped into the basket, then lower it down. Whenever Minh and Thành witnessed Công's exploits, they'd scamper away, fearing the wrath of the ants and the ensuing days of itching. Yet Công remained unruffled, holding the pole steady as the ants emerged from the nest, desperate for escape. Soon, they'd clamber onto the four strings suspending the basket, then onto the bamboo pole, advancing towards Công. But just as they neared his grasp, he'd tap the bamboo pole lightly, sending vibrations that caused them to tumble to the ground. In their panic, the ants scattered in all directions.

Then the two kids dared to gather around Công to watch him remove a few guava leaves from the ant nest, collecting their eggs, which resembled grains of cooked white rice. They then tagged along with Công to go fishing. Công didn't like the idea because they kept playing around and scaring away the fish, as Công often scolded them. But sometimes, because it was Công's responsibility to look after his younger brother, he reluctantly took Thành along. And if there was Thành, there had to be Minh.

Công brought along a round bamboo basket to hold the fish he caught. It was just half the size of the baskets that ladies carried with them to the market every morning. Arriving at his favorite fishing spot, on a smooth patch of land by the pond's edge, under the cool shade of a gooseberry tree, he sat down to bait the hook with ant eggs using a tiny fishing hook specialized for catching gourami fish. He raised his eyebrows, pinpointing the spot to cast his line, slowly lowering the bait into the water, ensuring it hit the familiar secret location where he knew there were plenty of fish. He sat still, eyes fixed on the bobbing garlic stem used as a float. When the float sank, he jerked the rod up. Every time, without fail, there was a wriggling gourami fish at the end of the fishing line. Công removed the fish, placing it in the bamboo basket, and submerged it in the water to keep the fish alive until he brought it home. So, for dinner that evening at Thành's house, there was crispy fried fish with spicy fish sauce, deliciously prepared.

As Thành and Minh reminisced about the fun-filled fishing expeditions with Công, he appeared. With nothing pressing inside the house, Công wandered out to stand before the door, relishing the coolness beneath the tamarind tree. Observing the two friends playing under its shade, he couldn't help but shake his head. "You two are already entering high school, yet you still act like children."

In truth, the two, now on the cusp of adolescence, had begun to outgrow their old pastimes, including the once-addictive games of their younger years. Sensing the shift, Thành extended an invitation to Minh to explore his backyard and collect sap from the 'Trôm' (Tropical chestnut) tree.

Since arriving at Thành's rustic country home, Minh found himself continually captivated by the surrounding scenery. Each moment seemed to unveil a new marvel, from the exposed roots of trees reaching skyward to the scuttling wind-crabs traversing the muddy fields, and even the peculiar fish capable of climbing trees and darting through the swamp.

Now, as they ventured towards the Sterculia (Trôm) tree, a species previously unknown to Minh, his sense of wonder only deepened. The 'Trôm' tree in Thành's yard is as big as a small mango tree behind Minh's garden. Its leaves are long, almost like mango leaves, but they spread out like the wings of a parachute at the end of each branch. At first glance, there's nothing particularly eye-catching about it, but when Thành led Minh to the base of the tree and showed him the pieces of resin-like gum embedded in the rough bark, along with the many scars, Minh found it strange. Thành pulled out a piece of milky-white resin, speckled with black dust from the tree bark, and handed it to Minh to see.

"That's 'Trôm' sap, bled from the cuts on the tree trunk that you saw. It can be soaked in water to make a refreshing beverage," Thành explained, before taking Minh inside the house to show him several pieces of dried, hardened 'Trôm' sap stored in a small box. Thành then poured for Minh a glass of Trôm sap refreshment from a large jar. Taking a sip of the thick, jelly-like drink, Minh felt a refreshing coolness, reminiscent of morning dew, coupled with the sweet taste of alum sugar. It was yet another delightful surprise for Minh.

Truly, it was a remarkable gift from nature. In coastal regions where the water tastes salty, rendering tamarind sour and other fruits like guava bitter, the availability of 'Trôm' sap offers a welcome respite. Providing cooling and refreshing drinks, it serves as a small but significant comfort for those enduring the relentless challenges of coastal living.

5. "Rat"

Unfortunately, the relatively tranquil days in southern Vietnam after the country's split swiftly faded away. The armed conflict between the North and the South began to intensify with the arrival of the first American troops in Đà Nẵng in the mid-1960s, and the war escalated ever since. Although it initially unfolded in remote areas with unfamiliar names, the signs of war soon permeated urban neighborhoods. One could witness these signs through the sight of a hearse during the day or the haunting sound of bamboo tocsin from a funeral echoing through the night. Gradually, these tocsin sounds evolved from a singular monotony, which could lead a concerned individual to a specific house in the neighborhood, evoking sorrow for those left behind - perhaps an elderly mother or a young wife with several children. Now, numerous bamboo tocsin prayers rise simultaneously from various places, becoming incessant and spanning the entire neighborhood.

In the midst of the raging battlefields, the Saigon rear drifted along with the music, overshadowing the sounds of gunfire and bombs. The romantic melodies imported from the North during the 1954 migration viewed the war through rose-colored glasses, gentle and buoyant like steps on clouds that no longer seemed appropriate. From then on, the music became more worldly and matter-of-fact, with lyrics like "A person dies twice, their flesh torn in pieces," or a soldier "returning, perhaps in a coffin adorned with flowers, or on a stretcher..." Or he may return "a defeated, crippled general."

The impoverished communities, on the other hand, seek solace in the poignant melodies of classical songs, finding respite from their troubles. Many residents in these neighborhoods already own a radio, no longer needing to congregate at the front gate of a richer man to tune in. The traditional melancholic tunes echo throughout the day, spanning from the start to the end of the alleys, ingraining themselves in the hearts of even the youngest listeners.

"Tomorrow is someone's wedding,
Why is Phà Ca, the tribal girl, feeling blue?"

From the sentiments of the highland tribal girl to the sentiments of the sedge mat seller:

"This mat, I won't sell it, searching for you but not finding...
Oh... searching for you but not finding, I lay my head on the pillow
every night."
"The mat boat from Cà Mau has anchored on the shore of Ngã Bảy,
why doesn't the girl from years past come out to greet?"

The voices of Thanh Nga, Út Bạch Lan, and Út Trà Ôn at times soar high into the depths of the sky, then descend low to touch the thick earth. Listening again and again, day and night, one can still feel their touch deep in the heart.

Outside, on the streets, amidst the harmonious glow of colorful lights illuminating the universe, echoes the melodious voice of Thái Thanh, stirring the souls of mountains and rivers, resonating with joyful melodies alongside every step of the caravan on the Cái Quan road. The singing revitalizes the footsteps of exploration, expands horizons, and stirs confidence through the splendor of bygone glory. If that is the call for sunrise from the sunflower's silently lamenting the endless night, then within the corners of the dance hall lies the heart's voice of a wandering rose in the mist, embracing the dream of dawn that only exists in reminiscence.

Outside, on the boulevard, immersed in the sparkling lights illuminating the universe, the resounding voice of Thái Thanh filled the air, echoing the soul of rivers and mountains and resonating with joyous melodies following each step of the pioneer's marching procession on the main road to the South - Con Đường Cái Quan. The singing brought to life the steps of exploration, expanding horizons, and arousing belief through the radiance of a bygone era.

If that was the call of the sunflower silently reproaching the endless night, then in the corner of the dance floor, the heartbeat was the voice of a wandering rose in the mist, embracing dreams of dawn that existed only in memories. The enchanting voice of Thanh Thúy filled countless glasses with wine, toasting to pilots after night flights, soldiers just separated from fallen comrades on the battlefield, or lonely individuals trying to forget in the haze of alcohol and cigarette smoke. It was a delicate voice that encapsulated the entire essence of Vietnamese women - steeped in hidden sorrows, yet enduring without complaints through generations.

In the Myrtle Tree neighborhood, even though many people may not be acquainted, everyone knows about Mrs. Bảy's family, whom many casually refer to as 'Mrs. Betel' because her mouth always chews on betel leaf. Encountering her anywhere, whether she's busy cooking rice next to her leafy shelter, or wandering the streets searching for her two children who work as laborers for some wealthy families in the area, as soon as she greets you, you'll see her fidgeting towards a clump of trees, bushes by the roadside, or a ditch, bending down as if searching for something dropped on the ground, then stretching her neck far to spit off a piece of betel residue.

Neighbors who come to see "Mrs. Betel" usually just want to call on one of her two children to help with chores. After Mr. Bảy, her husband, died in the attack on the French outpost on the outskirts of Saigon, she remained single to raise her two young children, "Pig" and "Rat." "Pig" is a brother a year older than his sister "Rat." These unusual names, based on their birth years in the zodiac, were chosen in the hope that malevolent spirits would be deterred by the ugly names and not take her children away. This was the explanation given by "Mrs. Betel" whenever someone, out of curiosity or with a hint of reproach, asked her why she had given her children such "inhuman" names.

It seemed that Heaven did not disappoint her, as "Pig" and "Rat" both grew up healthy and reached adulthood, despite living from hand to mouth. When they fell ill, they would curl up on the plank bed, cover themselves with a blanket, and endure, praying that the next day would be better than the last, since they could not afford doctors or medicine.

When 'Pig' was eight years old, he started working as a courier for his father's friends involved in the resistance against the French. Occasionally, they asked 'Pig' to deliver messages between members of the organization, such as letters or verbal messages. Initially, he didn't realize he was working for the resistance because the messages were often vague, like "Hello uncle, the ducks have eaten all the rice," or "Grandpa invites you for a drink," even though his grandparents had long passed away.

However, he enjoyed meeting his father's friends because whenever they returned from the Bàn Cờ district, they always remembered to bring him a bag of candy they called Bàn Cờ candy. His favorite was the white candy with red stripes that melted sweetly in his mouth. He never questioned why his father's friends, who had come all the way from the countryside to Saigon, always went to Bàn Cờ. He didn't know that the slum area in Bàn Cờ was a hub for the anti-French resistance. He was too young to understand.

Even the candy seemed like a gift from heaven to him. His father, when alive, used to worry that eating too much candy would spoil 'Pig's' appetite, so he often hid the sweets. Occasionally, to reward 'Pig', his father would secretly take a piece of candy and hide it in his hand, then lead 'Pig' to pray at the altar. Pretending to reach up to the altar, his father would "summon" the candy from heaven and give it to him. 'Pig' would happily accept the heavenly treat, though he had a nagging feeling that something wasn't quite right.

By the time he was fifteen, he had no doubts left about the origin of the candy treats, and he readily answered the call of his country, joining the resistance with his father's friends. From then on, Mrs. 'Betel' lived alone with 'Rat' in a tattered hut by the river, running errands, doing maid services, and performing other manual labor to make ends meet.

In the Gooseberry neighborhood, there was a man named Phong. After two years of honing his English at the Vietnam-America Society, he worked as an interpreter for a few years, and had already built a new house and bought a scooter. Yesterday, Phong was riding his Vespa out of his house when he saw 'Rat' carrying a basket to the market to buy groceries for Miss Út, a wealthy lady in the area. He waved 'Rat' over to start a conversation. Phong mentioned that he knew a bar owner who was looking for help with washing and ironing clothes. It was a stable job, unlike 'Rat''s current situation where she had to take on odd jobs around the neighborhood whenever someone called on her.

Although 'Rat' had never seen a bar, she had heard of them. She thought her mother would not approve of her working in such a place, so she gave a noncommittal response to Phong. Since yesterday, Phong's suggestion had been lingering in 'Rat''s mind, weaving dreams of earning money to support her mother and even buying her the delicacies that 'Rat' had seen in wealthy households. 'Rat' suddenly thought of asking Miss Út for advice. Miss Út was a young woman in the neighborhood whom 'Rat' admired like an older sister, as she often helped her and her mother in times of need. Additionally, she knew that her mother held Miss Út in high regard. If Miss Út approved, she believed her mother would likely agree as well.

Sitting under the Muntingia (fish-egg) tree in front of the house, Miss Út frowned as she listened to 'Rat' talk about Phong suggesting a job at a bar. Hearing the word "bar" and thinking of 'Rat''s young age and naive nature, warning bells instinctively rang in Miss Út's head, much like a protective mother or, in this case, an older sister safeguarding her younger sibling.

"Normally, I would have immediately told you 'No'," Miss Út said, "but since Phong seems like a decent person from a respectable family, I don't know what to say."

"I've heard people talk about various things regarding those bars. But I've known Phong since we were kids, so I don't think he would dupe me."

"He probably wouldn't deceive you. I'm just worried that in such a chaotic place, it might be hard for a young girl like you to stay safe."

"If I ask my mom about this, she probably won't agree. But, as you know, staying around here I won't be able to make enough money to care for her. For almost a year now, thanks to the medicine you provided that my mom has been able to hold on. We can't just keep asking you for your support for ever."

"I understand your situation, but life isn't just about money. I've had opportunities before, like renting cars to Americans or taking laundry contracts with the American military, but I turned them all down. We've lived through the French and Japanese eras and witnessed many lives, like moths flocking to a flame, only to be burned in the end. I'm not blaming anyone; everyone has their own circumstances. I just want to say that if we can avoid something, we should."

"I know. So what should we do now?"

"If it's like Phong said, a stable job is good. Maybe after saving up for a while, you can find something else to do."

"Alright, I'll ask my mom for permission. I'll tell her I've consulted with you."

"Be sure to take care of yourself. Don't follow others' bad examples. You're there to do laundry, so focus on your work. Let others do as they will. Everyone has their own life."

"I understand."

Miss Út still wasn't reassured:

"We're poor, but we need to maintain our dignity. Think about how sad your mom would be if there were any scandal..."

"I understand what you mean. I'll remember your advice."

The next day, Miss Út personally altered one of her 'bà ba' shirts for Rat to wear when she went with Phong to meet the bar owner.

"Hey, Sister Thúy, this is Rat from the neighborhood I mentioned to you a few days ago," Phong said, introducing Rat to Thúy, the bar owner who, despite being in her forties, looked like she was in her thirties with all the heavy makeup.

"Wow, how clever of you, knowing that I needed someone today."

As she spoke, Thúy glanced at 'Rat' from head to toe. She was slightly surprised by 'Rat''s pleasant face despite the lack of makeup. Her slender figure showcased a well-proportioned body.

"Are you someone's sweetheart?"

'Rat' raised her eyebrows, trying to understand Thuy's question, but couldn't figure it out. She looked down at the ground and mumbled:

"No, why do you ask?"

Thúy reached out and touched the front hem of Rat's dress, then said, "Do you know how much this type of fabric costs? If no one were supporting you, you wouldn't be able to afford this. And if you could afford this, you wouldn't need to work."

Realizing what Thúy meant, Rat quickly responded, "This dress was lent to me by Miss Út in the neighborhood."

Turning to Phong, Thúy remarked:

"She's so pretty, and you call her 'Rat'? It takes away her charm."

Thúy scrutinized 'Rat' again from top to bottom.

"Tell me, in your family, what's your birth order?"

"I'm the sixth child, ma'am," 'Rat' responded, counting all her siblings dead and alive.

"Then I'll call you 'Sáu' (or Sixth) for convenience, okay?"

Before Thúy could finish her sentence, a waitress hurriedly ran in, urging her to go to the front to deal with an arising situation: a group of new customers had shown up and there were not enough hostesses to greet them. Thúy quickly hired 'Rat' and sent her to the back to assist Mrs. Tư with the laundry.

Not longer than a week after 'Rat' was hired to do the laundry at 'Sister' Thúy's bar, one afternoon, a group of American soldiers on leave suddenly crowded into the bar. With a shortage of hostesses, Thúy was flustered, trying to keep the customers from leaving and missing out on potential earnings. She was at a loss, as today two staff members had called in sick with the flu. Thúy stepped to the back, feeling troubled, and pulled up a stool next to the dining table, sipping her unfinished iced coffee while thinking of a solution.

Glancing toward the backyard, she saw 'Rat' sitting by the bathroom, washing clothes on the cement floor, her pants rolled up to her knees, revealing her slender, fair legs. Despite coming from a poor family and having to work from a young age, 'Rat's natural beauty shone through. An idea flashed in Thúy's mind - an idea that had actually been simmering ever since she noticed the occasional glimpses of feminine charm in 'Rat,' or shall we say 'Sáu,' as she would be known around the bar now.

"Sáu, what are you doing? Come here, I need to talk to you."

"I'm washing clothes," 'Rat' replied, standing up and wiping the soapy water from her bare arms into the basin. She quickly dried her hands on her pant legs, slipping on her wooden clogs, and hurried over to stand before Thúy.

"Yes, sister Thúy, you called for me?"

"Yeah, I have something to talk to you about... Lately, first Hồng took leave, and now Thủy is sick and can't come to work. Thủy really knows how to pick a time to be off. Just when the bar is crowded like these days, she's at home. I was thinking, maybe you could help me out."

'Rat' didn't understand Thúy's intention and looked at her questioningly,

"What do you need help with, sister?"

"I mean, I'd like you to take Thủy's place for a bit."

'Rat' was taken aback, nervously refusing,

"I can't do that, I'm scared. If my mom finds out, she'll scold me to death."

Thúy, experienced and anticipating 'Rat''s reaction, quickly replied,

"You don't have to worry. You won't be doing anything wrong. You'll just be hanging around the lobby, entertaining the customers like the others do every day. There's nothing to be afraid of."

Seeing 'Rat' bowing her head, avoiding her gaze, fidgeting with her shirt hem, showing signs of awkwardness and uncertainty, Thúy confided:

"There have been some issues around here lately, so I turned to you for help. You know, doing business nowadays isn't easy."

Thúy gestured toward the colorful array of clothes hanging all over the clothesline, and continued:

"Just a few months ago, the girls still had to take these clothes home and wash them themselves. It's only recently, thank goodness, that our bar has been a bit busier, and they complained about not having time to do laundry anymore. So I asked Phong to introduce a reliable person to help..." Thúy's voice trailed off as she observed 'Rat's' hesitation. Thúy lifted her coffee cup, took a sip to moisten her voice, and then continued:

"According to what Phong told me, your family is going through a tough time, and your mom is sick. That's why I asked Phong to call you over for a trial. I'm letting you know in advance, if things go smoothly with the business, I could have you stay here and help me permanently. I'll pay you a monthly salary. Around mid-month, I'll give you a little advance to manage, and at the end of the month, I'll give you the rest of your salary."

'Rat''s heart suddenly pounded with excitement. No feeling could surpass this; no joy could be greater. The two words "monthly salary," though 'Rat' heard them for the first time, she understood their meaning. It was something unimaginable for 'Rat'. It was beyond her wildest dreams. Until now, 'Rat' had only been paid for odd jobs she performed, with the payers treating the money as if it were a gift of their generosity. The largest amount 'Rat' had ever received was no more than five 'đồng' (Vietnamese piaster), which was the payment for a full day's hard work, usually from dawn till dusk. Even though it was a daily wage, it wasn't a fixed amount; it depended on the goodwill of the homeowner. Sometimes, receiving only 3 or 4 piasters, 'Rat' would still bow her head, thanking the homeowner with a radiant smile before leaving. If, on rare occasions, the homeowner asked for the rate she would charge for her labor, 'Rat' would answer, as taught by her mother, "Sir/Madame, whatever you want to give." As Mrs. 'Betel' taught her, "You have to say that to make the homeowner feel appreciated. Next time when there's work, they'll remember you and call on you again."

Recalling the first time 'Rat' held a five-piaster note in her hand, her initial thought was about being able to buy five poor-man fish sandwiches. As the name suggested, these sandwiches were made with the tomato sauce left over in the sardine can, not the sardines themselves. Even that, it's a rare treat that she or her mother can afford.

Lost in thought about her circumstances and her sick mother waiting for her to bring back money for medicine, 'Rat' found it hard to resist the allure of changing her life through Thúy's offer. Despite her youth, 'Rat' had started working early and dealt with many people. She couldn't ignore the implied warning in Thúy's words about the instability of her current job if she didn't listen. Knowing this, 'Rat' still hesitated and made excuses:

"But sis, I don't even have a long dress (traditional Vietnamese 'áo dài') to wear outside. And even if I go out there, I wouldn't know what to say to the customers. Until now, I haven't known how to talk to anyone, let alone foreigners. I don't know their language."

Quietly celebrating her successful persuasion, Thúy quickly responded:

"It's not difficult at all. You just sit out there, have a drink, and befriend the customers, like the other girls do. You don't have to say much. I know everyone is a bit awkward at first, so I'll have Đông, the bartender, keep an eye on you. If you need anything, just ask him. He'll help you. Don't worry."

Thúy stood up, warmly grasping Rat's hand. "Alright then, go hang the laundry and come up to my room. I'll find a proper dress for you. In this house, we may lack some things, but we don't lack clothes. Don't worry about it."

Rat reluctantly nodded. "Yes, sis," she said, then went out to the backyard to hang the clothes. Thúy returned to her office, picked up the phone, and called Hồng. Hồng had asked for two days off to take care of her three-year-old son, who had a high fever and needed to be taken to the hospital.

After a few inquiries and hearing that Hồng's son's condition had improved somewhat, Thúy asked her to take a taxi and come right away to prepare 'Rat'. "Before sending her out to battle," Thúy joked, bursting into laughter. As she hung up the phone, Thúy called Aunt Tư to come and do Rat's nails.

After hanging up the remaining clothes, 'Rat' nervously took heavy steps back into the house, tiptoeing into Thúy's bedroom where 'Rat' had always freely come and gone to take dirty clothes for washing. But today, 'Rat''s heart was filled with a vague worry, feeling like she was about to do something she probably shouldn't. Thúy caught sight of 'Rat' and quickly called out, "Come here, look at this." As she spoke, Thúy pointed towards the four brightly colored 'áo dài' (traditional Vietnamese long dresses) spread out on the edge of the bed, comparing sizes to see which one would fit 'Rat' the best. Pointing to the purple dress, Thúy said:

"This one belongs to Hồng. I think its size should fit you. Try it on and see if it fits. If it's tight, try the blue one from Thủy; it's a bit wider, but the length should be fine since both of them are about your height. Remember to try on Hồng's white muslin pants too, to see if they need any adjustments. Then sit here and wait for Hồng to come; she'll take care of everything for you. Poor little Hồng, she's busy at home but still trying to come and take care of you. I have to go greet the guests for a bit; they won't be happy if they don't see me."

Sitting alone in the luxurious room filled with the silks of the fortunate cocoons born in the serene celestial silk, reeking of expensive perfume, 'Rat' thought absentmindedly while glancing around the room. In front of 'Rat', beside the mother-of-pearl inlaid divan, was an old iron safe with a few patches of peeling green paint. On top of it sat a small incense burner and several large incense sticks smoldering in offering to the god of wealth. Next to it was a vanity table, cluttered with colorful lipsticks, powder boxes, perfume bottles, and eyebrow pencils. In the corner of the table was a hair dryer bought from a U.S. military PX, alongside many hair rollers, several large and small combs, and hairbrushes. In front of the mirror were two foreign candy boxes filled with jewelry, including many pearl necklaces, earrings, chains, and various rings.

After looking around, 'Rat' dejectedly gazed down at the four 'áo dài' sprawled across the bed, like four careless girls surrendering to fate after a wild revelry. 'Rat' wearily stood up, hesitantly following Thúy's instructions, awkwardly changing into Hồng's clothes. Glancing at herself in the mirror, 'Rat' felt embarrassed and awkward, quickly returning to sit on the edge of the bed, as if to distance herself from the strange, uncertain world named 'Sáu', and find solace in the familiar, safe world of 'Rat', her true self.

In that world, beauty and delicious food were not for 'Rat' to enjoy, but to care for 'Miss Hai'. Since childhood, 'Rat' had worked at the district chief's house, often doing small chores like dusting furniture, cleaning the betel tray, or washing the lime pot for his wife. However, 'Rat's' main job was washing clothes for Phượng, the district chief's beloved granddaughter, whom 'Rat' called 'Miss Hai'. Additionally, every afternoon, 'Rat' would peel oranges or wash fruit in the kitchen, waiting for Phượng to wake up from her nap, so she could bring it up to her bedroom and 'invite Miss Hai to eat'. Occasionally, fearing that Phượng might get pimples from eating too many oranges, as the district chief's wife believed, she would send 'Rat' to the market to buy jicama to peel for Phượng due to its cooling properties.

Over the years of living alongside and serving the district chief's wife and closely attending to 'Miss Hai' Phượng, 'Rat' had become more than just a loyal servant. She felt like a part of the family, contributing to maintaining a way of life, a tradition passed down from generation to generation.

For so long, 'Rat' had contentedly contributed to building a paradise without herself in it, simply because there seemed to be no better choice. Today, for the first time in her life, she could determine her own destiny, which inevitably brought about a sense of unease. She feared the risks that awaited her and the deep-seated prejudices that had bound individuals for generations, yet she also felt exhilarated at the threshold of an open future, where she could freely express herself and move forward. Ultimately, the allure of self-discovery was powerful enough for her to embrace all the consequences of this fateful choice.

Several months later, Thúy's bar was completely deserted. Rat had worried that this day would come. Outside, the rain still drizzled lightly. Rat hastily put on the Hong Kong raincoat that Thúy's friend had persuaded her to buy the month before, then sped off on her Honda to meet Miss Út.

Miss Út asked, "Why do you look so nervous?"

Cautiously looking around, Rat leaned in and whispered in Miss Út's ear, "Tomorrow, I'm quitting my job for good."

Although Miss Út had anticipated this day, she still empathized with Rat's anxiety. She gently inquired, "What are your plans then?"

"Fortunately, as you know, with your help, I've managed to save a little over the past two years. I hope we can manage whatever comes our way," Rat replied, uncertain of what lay ahead.

Miss Út comforted her, "Well, back then, you didn't even have a penny. Your family all managed to get by somehow."

After a moment of contemplation, Miss Út continued, "To be honest, I'm somewhat happy for you. Maybe this change will be for the better. With the money you've saved up until now, you have over ten thousand dollars, enough to start a small business. Your mom would be happy too. Lucky for you she didn't find out what you did in these past few months; otherwise, she would have disowned you."

Miss Út reached for the key on the desk, walked into the bedroom, opened her safe, and took out the money that Rat had entrusted to her. Sitting by the edge of the bed, Miss Út handed Rat an old biscuit box, filled with stacks of green dollar bills and some red ones, along with a few silver dollars she received from some American soldiers. In total, it was nearly twelve thousand dollars. Miss Út made Rat count every dollar meticulously. Watching Rat nervously handle such a large sum of money, Miss Út felt worried again and reiterated her previous advice:

"Do you remember how I always told you to save money? When you have enough capital, you can start a business."

"Yes, that's why I haven't spent much. Just occasionally buying little things for my mom. I remember you said once I have enough money, you'd help me find a place to start a business. Have you found one?"

"I know someone who is renting out the ground floor of an appartment by the riverbank. What do you think?"

"I don't know what to think, sis. Please figure it all out for me."

"That place is right in the middle of the town, near two or three schools, so I've been thinking lately that opening a 'bazaar' selling school supplies might work. Nowadays, schools are popping up everywhere, and you see students and teachers everywhere you go."

'Rat' beamed at the thought of being a shop owner, but then shook her head at the reality.

"I don't think I can do it, sis. I don't know anything about running a business. I can barely read, how could I manage the trade... I can count money, sure, but I have no idea how to make a profit."

"Alright, I'll help you taking care of the business at first. You'll learn as you go, it's not that hard."

After a moment of contemplation, Miss Út added, "Remember not to waste your money, dear. As the saying goes, 'If you keep eating while not working, even a mountain will collapse'.

Leaving Miss Út, 'Rat' carried a mix of emotions, both happy and sad. She felt sad because she had lost her job and the nightly earnings that came with it, facing the uncertainty of the days and months ahead. Yet, there was also a sense of relief, as if a burden had been lifted from her shoulders. Every day at work, 'Rat' felt the heavy weight of worrying about her mother finding out about her actual job at the bar.

As she neared her home, 'Rat' silently hoped that Mrs. 'Betel' was busy cooking dinner, giving 'Rat' a chance to hide the money. Entering the house and not seeing her mother, 'Rat' assumed she was cooking in the back. She carefully tucked the stacks of money under the foam mattress where she slept every night, smoothing out the bedsheet afterward. After scrutinizing the bed for any signs that someone could detect, 'Rat' stepped out to look for Mrs. 'Betel', still unsure whether to tell her about losing her job.

Eventually, she knew she had to tell her, but she worried it might upset her mother if she did it too soon. Suddenly, 'Rat' saw her mother lying on the old bamboo bed behind the house, the rice cooker cold without any firewood. Startled, 'Rat' exclaimed, "Oh, Mom, are you sick?"

Mrs. 'Betel' lay curled up, facing the wall, not responding to 'Rat''s inquiries. 'Rat' grew more worried and tried to shake her mother awake, asking urgently, "Mom, are you okay? Should I take you to the hospital?"

Mrs. 'Betel' weakly pushed 'Rat' away, saying, "Stop pretending to care. You want me dead so you can be happy."

'Rat' was taken aback. "What are you saying, Mom?"

Mrs. 'Betel' remained silent. 'Rat' felt a sense of foreboding, sensing that something had made her mother very angry, unlike previous times when she would just scold and forget. 'Rat' tried to inquire further, "Why are you saying such strange things when everything seemed fine?"

Mrs. 'Betel' replied bitterly, "Go ask the neighbors."

Wiping her tears with a towel from the bedside, Mrs. 'Betel' choked up, "The whole neighborhood says you're dating an American."

The world seemed to collapse. Legs trembling, 'Rat' slumped down by the edge of the bed, burying her face in tears.

Earlier in the day, Aunt Tám from the neighborhood, who was preparing for her son's wedding, had come by to ask 'Rat' to help with housework over the weekend. Upon entering the house and seeing the neatly made bed with pink sheets next to the brightly polished glass buffet, Aunt Tám sneered and remarked to Mrs. 'Betel', "Well, it seems like 'Rat' has hit the jackpot with an American. Haven't seen her much lately. I was thinking of asking her to help out for a few days, but with her new lifestyle, it's probably not going to happen."

With those words, Aunt Tám left, leaving a piercing stab deep in Mrs. 'Betel''s heart. She felt both pity and blame towards her daughter. Pity because deep down, she knew, "My daughter is doing this for me." At the same time, she felt her daughter was too naive. Mrs. 'Betel' would rather die with a clear conscience and reunite with her husband than live and endure the gossip of society.

'Rat' wiped her tears, apologizing to her mother and attributing everything to fate. She recounted the story of a sick colleague and the employer's request for her to fill in, which she couldn't refuse. 'Rat' avoided mentioning that she wanted to make money quickly to be able to buy medicine for Mrs. 'Betel' while she was seriously ill, fearing her mother would be saddened. Mrs. 'Betel' refused to leave the bed, skipping dinner and retreating into sleep.

'Rat' collapsed onto the empty bed amidst the desolate island. She was restless, unable to close her eyes, feeling as if all her efforts were futile. She realized it was all an illusion, suddenly disappearing like the colors of a rainbow vanishing in the blink of an eye after the burst of a water bubble. From the feeling of freedom like a bird soaring high while riding her Honda on deserted roads, to the sensation of pride in her own worth through the praise of her employer, or after every time she held a thick wad of dollar bills given by the bar owner. Although she had long resigned herself to living in the dreamlike world within the thick walls of prejudice, it didn't release her. It continued to tighten its grip until it shattered her small bag of dreams. She felt suffocated in the long, restless nights illuminated by a flickering oil lamp. Out of habit, 'Rat' reached for the bottle of oil on the bedside table, intending to refill the lamp, but felt it was meaningless. She didn't need the light to scrutinize her private life; she wanted to find peace in the darkness of the night. 'Rat' placed the oil bottle back on the table. The bottle of antibiotic pills lay unused next to it, staring at her. 'Rat' looked at it intently, motionless, contemplative, and as if she had found a way to escape, she bravely emptied the remaining pills into her hand, poured them into her mouth, and lay back on the bed. Satisfied in her own private world. By noon, when Mrs. 'Betel' heard no movement from inside, it was too late. She entered the room, hugged her lifeless child, crying bitterly.

Miss Út sat alone under the shade of the Muntingia tree in front of her home, once the favored spot for 'Rat' to confide her little secrets. As she sat, occasionally shaking her head, she couldn't help but contemplate the loss of 'Rat.' In the quiet of the moment, echoes of her father's melodic voice reciting poetry from the veranda lingered in her ears, a poignant reminder of the passage of time:

"When the heavens and earth stirred up a dusty wind,
Many a red-cheeked guest bore burdens aplenty;
Heaven beyond the deep blue above,
For whose sake were these troubles wrought?"

6. The Drifting Water Hyacinth

Tuất [twət], a Vietnamese-Canadian man in his forties, embodies a captivating blend of dark complexion and robust, tall stature. There's an unmistakable aura of mindfulness that surrounds him, drawing the attention of all those he encounters. Not long ago, Tuất, like many other Vietnamese refugees, found himself akin to tropical trees violently uprooted by a sudden storm, cast into the vast unknown of the sea. They drifted to a cold and distant corner of the Earth, faced with the stark choice of survival or perishing in an unfamiliar environment of alien soil, water, and climate.

The catastrophic collapse of South Vietnam, Tuất's homeland, heralded a seismic shift in the annals of history for an entire nation. The enormity of this transformation was so profound that Tuất and his fellow countrymen, swept up in the eleventh-hour exodus from the war-torn land, grappled to grasp its full implications, feeling adrift in a disorienting reverie. The past slipped away like grains of sand through their fingers, and the present blurred into a nebulous and uncertain future.

Arriving in the new country felt like stepping onto an icy island amidst an expanse of endless white snow for Tuất. Everything appeared utterly unfamiliar, from the ethereal clouds drifting in the sky to the frost-kissed branches and grass on the ground. Even the distant voices and laughter echoing from the crowd, juxtaposed with the mechanical hum of passing vehicles, felt alien in their own way.

Yet, fueled by determination and tireless effort, after less than a decade of settling in Canada, Tuất and his wife achieved the remarkable feat of owning a nail salon in the heart of downtown

Winnipeg, Manitoba. He attributes his ability to adapt and grow in the foreign land to the kindness of the host country, but also to the sacred gift from his grandmother while he was still an infant: a moral compass.

This morning presents a rare and precious opportunity for reverie to unfold before Tuất. The remnants of a snowstorm from the previous night had deterred the usual influx of customers, unveiling the enchantment of the fluffy white snow blanketing the earth around him. It beckoned him into a realm of introspection, allowing him to drift back to cherished memories of times gone by.

Tuất enters the office tucked away at the rear of the nail shop, sinking into a chair and casually propping his feet up on piles of receipts, large and small, scattered across the desk. Absentmindedly, he gazes through the glass window, yearning for a few moments of precious escapism. Soon, he reaches out to the cassette player nestled in the corner of the table, initiating a ritual: when the shop is devoid of customers, he indulges in Vietnamese music, allowing its melodies to serenade his soul.

The enchanting voice of Diva Hương Lan permeates the room, beckoning Tuất to unlock his heart and welcome the stirring harmonies. The dulcet tones carry him away to a realm of dreams, where solace is found and memories blossom. Oh, Diva Hương Lan's singing! It's akin to a gentle breeze swaying a hammock amidst the summer heat, beneath the verdant canopy of the mangosteen trees in Lái Thiêu gardens. It evokes the image of a riverboat, delivering fresh water to the eagerly awaited denizens along the banks of the Saltwater Canal.

The music conjures visions of crimson, luscious plums, reminiscent of the rosy cheeks of a vendor girl stationed behind a fruit stall at the bustling bus stop, Trung Lương, at the entrance to the western rice fields. It brings forth the imagery of white storks gracefully soaring into the distance as the bus departs from Bình Điền Bridge, journeying toward the Mekong delta region.

And then, there's the memory of a small glass of juice crafted from the sap of the Trôm tree (Sterculia foetida), delicately infused with alum sugar, a revitalizing elixir bestowed by a lover that instantly invigorated the heart of a soldier in training at a military camp. Drifting along the river of dreams to the tune of Hương Lan's singing, the expansive sky unfurls, enveloping the warm sunshine of the homeland that suddenly surges forth, embracing the very essence of Tuất's soul.

Outside Tuất's office, everything is engulfed in a sea of dazzling white snow. Snow blankets the ground, adorns fences, and embraces tree trunks in the harsh winter. Strangely, the frost doesn't chill the nostalgia for the homeland; instead, it warms up the childhood memories in Tuất's heart.

The blanket of white snow draping over the delicate apple branches brings to Tuất's mind the white netting that cradles the stems of water mimosa flourishing in the ponds and lakes of Long Kiến commune, Chợ Mới District, An Giang province— the very place where Tuất spent his childhood. Treasured memories surge forth, accompanied by the vivid taste of water mimosa infused with the savory essence of fish sauce in his grandmother's braised dish.

Tuất's mother's hometown was adjacent to his father's, situated on Ông Chưởng Islet, cradled by the Hậu River. This area was renowned for its abundance of fish and shrimp, to the extent that numerous birds would invite each other to partake in nature's bountiful feast, giving rise to a local folk song:

'Three times the crow tells the kite,

There are plenty of fish and shrimp left on Ông Chưởng Islet.'

Tuất was unsure about the exact abundance of fish, but the story his grandmother shared had made a lasting impression on him. During the high-water season, fish from Cambodia's Tonlé Sap Lake would cascade downstream, following the floodwaters to replenish the cultivated lands. Villagers would wade into the fields, collecting the fish to take home for drying or preserving as salted fish, known as pissalat. Carrying two baskets of fish suspended at each end of a yoke, and occasionally feeling the weight bearing down on their shoulders, they would pause to select the largest fish from each basket and discard them to lighten the load.

Thinking of salted fish brings back memories for Tuất, especially the sweet aroma of snakehead fish tails used to mellow the saltiness of the braised fish sauce, a dish savored with freshly harvested vegetables from around the house—a specialty his grandmother used to prepare whenever relatives visited. During those meals, she always made sure to set aside two succulent prawns from the dish and place them in Tuất's rice bowl, ensuring no other kids could snatch his favorite.

Every time Tuất reminisces about the past, the image of his grandmother invariably comes to mind. Although Tuất lived with his grandmother for only a few years during his early life, the river water continued to flow, unstoppable once set in motion, and the sediments continued to build, unmovable once deposited. The lullabies she sang to put him to sleep everynight continued to circulate in his bloodstream. The gentle and melodious sounds murmured in his subconscious, weaving a sky of magical childhood memories in Tuất's mind.

The verses and tunes at first were just jumbled thoughts in the child's mind:

... Horse, black horse pulling the golden carriage... The prince adorned his horse with all the golden and silver trappings, including decorative lotus flowers.

... Heading toward the royal palace, the prince escorted the princess home...

The words, the meanings, unfamiliar, were woven into images never seen, but for Tuất's heart, it was different. He tasted the sweetness in his grandmother's voice, felt the warmth, the gentleness, and the love emanating from her heart. And thus, he went to sleep in peace, lulled by the sound of the bells adorning the horse, seeking the wandering pink lotuses in the pond at his home.

The magical wonders gradually took root in the young soul. Somewhere deep in Tuất's subconscious were echoes of another sorrowful melody. It was played by the legendary Thạch Sanh, a strong and brave woodcutter, on his lute deep in a cave where his vicious half-brother had trapped him, intending to take credit for saving the lost princess.

Etched deep in Tuất's memory were also the fairy tales his grandmother told. Within this realm resided a girl named 'Tấm,' who had been killed by a wicked stepmother. Tấm, a gentle and filial soul, remained hidden within the core of a golden apple, hanging from a branch of the golden apple tree. Until the fateful day when she met a poor, lonely old lady standing under the tree and calling out,

"Gold apple, gold apple, fall into my sack, so this old lady can have a snack."

Tấm made her wish come true, and the old lady unknowingly took Tấm, hidden inside the golden apple, home. There, Tấm discreetly manifested herself during the times when the old lady was away, taking care of meals, cleaning, and tidying up the house for her.

Over time, through the folklores passed down by his grandmother, the ideals of good and bad, beauty and ugliness, virtue and vice, mirrored through contrasting characters in the legends, illuminated the path for Tuất, guiding him through life. This nurturing of his heart allowed him to understand both joy and sorrow, experiencing happiness as well as the sorrows of the country and the very land where his sacred umbilical cord was interred.

7. First Tết Overseas

The anticipation leading up to the first Tết (or Lunar New Year) for Vietnamese expatriates post-1975 is imbued with a sense of nostalgia, a blend of eager longing and restless anticipation. How could there still be any swallows heralding the arrival of Spring to dream of? How could there be the memorable New Year's Eve tradition of folding paper money into butterfly shapes, hanging them on the golden apricot branches adorning the altar, behind the shiny bronze candle holders, next to the offering fruit platter, next to the huge green watermelon? Here, days pass in a blur of waiting, with an undefined yearning for what awaits…

Is it the excitement of donning new attire? Or the eager anticipation of the first crackle of firecrackers, signaling the time to pay respects at the ancestral altar, lighting incense for New Year's offerings? Perhaps it's the simple pleasure of a game of cards with beloved siblings. Alternatively, is it the prospect of carefree leisure days, where worries are cast aside and thoughts dissolve, leisurely pedaling bicycles to visit teachers, friends, and cherished ones?

In this anticipation lies a tapestry of emotions, woven with threads of tradition, family, and the promise of cherished moments to come.

But, here, in the midst of North America, Spring suddenly emerges in the small hall beneath the church. Tết arrives unexpectedly amidst the gathering of fellow countrymen, each longing for the sound of Vietnamese whispers.

In Winnipeg, Reverend Swanson, despite having a name that many Vietnamese found difficult to pronounce correctly, endeared himself to the community and wholeheartedly supported the Vietnamese in organizing a Tết gathering in the church's basement banquet hall, marking the first New Year celebrated by Vietnamese refugees living overseas during the Year of the Dragon on Saturday, January 31, 1976.

A week before Tết, Hiển drove to pick up Tuất and Minh to go to Chinatown to buy candles and decorations for the Tết altar to create a festive atmosphere in the gathering room. Hiển was one of the earliest to own a car among the fellow countrymen at the time. He had previously studied telecommunication at the U.S. naval base on Treasure Island in San Francisco Bay, later returning as a trainer. Upon arriving in Winnipeg, due to his fluency in English and existing skills, he quickly found good employment and integrated into the local community, buying a car, purchasing a house, following the unwavering path guiding the lives of the immigrants on this land of opportunity.

As Hiển started the car, Tuất sat in the back seat, startled, looking around, searching. The familiar music that resonated daily from the radio at his workshop in Saigon, seemingly never to be heard again after several months of silence, suddenly emerged in the surroundings. It turned out to be coming from the cassette player in the front of Hiển's car - the tunes were not only familiar to the ears but also touched the depths of Tuất's heart.

The warmth emanating from the music melted the snow all around Tuất, turning it into a stream of sweet water - a cool spring trickling into his ears and touching his heart. The music from the cassette player embraced him completely. It was unmistakably the singing voice of the homeland's 'Sister of the Soldiers,' which Tuất used to hear every day on the radio and TV in Saigon. It was the voice of 'The Queen of TV,' Diva Phương Hồng Quế. To Tuất, that beloved voice felt even more intimate, carrying the affectionate tone of the friend he secretly loved and cherished.

The car finally came to a stop in front of the grocery store, pulling over to the side of the road. Minh, seated in the front, motioned to Hiển not to turn off the engine as he wanted to listen to the new song playing on the cassette. It was by his favorite singer, Diva Hà Thanh. From his parka pocket, Minh retrieved a pack of Player cigarettes and offered one to Hiển. The two of them cracked open the car window just slightly, enough to let the wisps of cigarette smoke drift out and prevent the cold from rushing in too quickly. For a brief moment, it felt as though even amidst the chill, they were transported back to the past, reminiscing on those rare moments when they sat together during breaks in their operations, surrounded by nature's embrace - whether beside the forest, by the field, or under the scorching tropical sky.

Only the enchantment of music, particularly Vietnamese music, had the power to summon phoenix blossoms in winter, golden apricot flowers on the white snow, soothing the ache in the soul, easing the pain in the hearts of those involuntary expatriates. Hà Thanh's singing infused the dignified beauty of the imperial palace into the depths of the Perfume River and the enduring affection of the Ngự mountains. If there were moments in the past her voice could offer peace and stillness in the midst of chaos, it was now, bringing the comforting lullaby of the homeland to those children lost in the upheaval of earth and heaven, reminding them of the extended history of the nation beyond the transient fluctuations of the world.

As the music subsided, Minh extinguished his cigarette and looked outside the window, musing:

- Thinking back, Phạm Quỳnh was only half right.

Hiển glanced at Minh expecting an explanation. Minh continued:

- The other day while we were having a drink, they recalled scholar Phạm Quỳnh's timeless saying, roughly... 'The Tale of Kiều remains... our nation remains.' But today I feel the need to add: Our music remains, our nation remains.

Hiển nodded in agreement. After a moment of contemplation, he spoke:

- True, very true. Haven't our music always be tied to the lives of the youth of every era?

Hiển was right. Enduring the ups and downs of the country, the Viet modern music, although born late, had become inseparable from the lives of urban youth, like a shadow following a figure through many decades. More importantly, it had penetrated the hearts of people and spread widely among the masses, overcoming all challenges from the difficult circumstances of the homeland to the societal prejudices against the profession of singers.

In each historical period, the joys and sorrows of the people gave rise to melodies and lyrics, encompassing a wide range of expressions, from gentle and romantic praises of love to strong and grand encouragements of patriotism, and from the melancholy of sharing the emotions of wartime youth to the restless pondering of life's purpose on this earth.

The three brothers entered the store to buy two packets of lucky money envelopes and some Tết votive candles. After that, Hiển said,

- Now I have to buy abalones too.

Tuất asked in surprise,

- Why is that, brother?

- Our ladies have been having headaches not knowing what to cook for the past few days.

- Well, for Tết we can just make braised meat and pickled vegetables, that's enough.

- The ladies are worried that people in Canada might not like it. Besides, they're not sure if the Canadians can stand the smell of our fish sauce.

- Oh, that makes sense, even though I've seen Americans in Vietnam gulp down fish sauce like anything, there are also those who scrunch up their noses, unable to bear that smell. So, what the ladies plan to do?

- They agree that traditional dishes, to some extent, must be served. Besides pickled vegetables with braised meat, there's also shrimp salad. But they still feel the need to have a more presentable dish to treat foreign guests. Fortunately, Aunty Bảy knows how to prepare abalones, so she suggested abalone dish.

- I've never heard of this dish for Tết.

- As long as it's an expensive dish, it's fine. Besides, Father Swanson gave us 50 dollars for Tết celebration. That's a lot. If we only cook braised meat, I am afraid there won't be enough pots to hold that much meat.

- Yeah, everyone is new here, and we do our best with whatever we can make.

- That's right. Aunty Hai wishes she had all the utensils to show off her skill in making square sticky rice cakes. But just take banana leaves alone, where can we find them? By the way, my wife asked me to go find rice papers for her to make fried spring rolls or some shrimp rolls. I gave up.

After buying two boxes of abalones, the three brothers went to buy two large poster papers, nearly half a yard wide, to draw a dragon and write 'Happy Tet Year of the Snake' to decorate the room and create a Tết atmosphere for the gathering.

Back at Hiển's house, everyone sat on the floor around the coffee table, equipped with two boxes of coloring crayons belonging to Hiển's son Tèo, rolled up their sleeves, and showcased their artistic talents. Tuất was praised for his beautiful handwriting and given a red board to write the Tết greetings. Minh and Hiển were in charge of drawing the dragon on a white board, based on the model that Hiển had prepared. It was an illustration for an article about Tết published in the Free Press newspaper.

After finishing, the three of them held up two posters, looking back and forth, looking horizontally and vertically. Hiển said:

- Why doesn't it look much like Tết?

Minh agreed,

- If only we bought two red posters, it would look more like Tết.

Tuất suddenly exclaimed,

- I know. Probably because we're missing red watermelon.

Anh Minh chuckled:

- This guy has a point. So this year, let's feed the Dragon some watermelon.

'Let's go for it,' Minh said and then held up a red wax stick, pointing to the dragon picture, asking for Hiển's opinion,

- Where do you think it's best to add watermelon to make it more interesting?

Tuất rolled on the floor laughing,

- I've never seen dragons eating watermelon before.

Minh slapped his forehead, exclaiming,

- How could I forget that! We need firecrackers too. Instead of lion dance firecrackers, let's play dragon dance firecrackers.

So the Dragon of 1976 was both eating watermelon and playing with... piles of red firecracker shells. But the three brothers were still not very satisfied. After emptying a can of Coca Cola, Hiển patted his thigh and said, 'I know, guys.'

- Tuất, it's your turn. Take the yellow crayon and fill the two cardboard pieces with yellow apricot blossoms for me.

Tuất eagerly got to work. Hiển smiled with delight. Minh sat still, gazing at the two masterpieces of painting for a moment and then nodded in approval,

- Now it really looks like Tết!

After finishing the two panels, Hiển looked at Minh and said,

- Minh, I want to talk to you about something.

- What is it?

- In the article about Tết in the newspaper, they call it the Chinese New Year. What do you think?

- I heard that the Chinese people came to Canada a long time ago. At least since the end of the 19th century. They came in groups. I heard it was a lot, to work as laborers building railways. Maybe because the locals have seen them celebrate Tết from that time until now, they are used to calling it that way.

- But now with us here, they can't say that.

- Our country is so small and tucked away across the ocean for anyone to notice.

- That's not quite true. The American press often used the term 'Tet Offensive' to refer to the attack during the Tết festival for the Year of the Monkey.

- Yeah, you're right. Come to think about it, even if people don't know, we should let people know.

- Completely agree. So, I'll go ahead and draft a letter from a reader to the journalist.

An hour later, the two brothers finished composing the draft. Hiển began typing on the typewriter a letter proposing to the Free Press newspaper to refer to Tết as the Lunar New Year, because it is the common new year day for several Asian communities, including the Vietnamese.

The first Tết of the Vietnamese diaspora after 1975 arrived amidst the excitement and nostalgia for home, after many restless days of waiting, not exactly knowing who or what they were waiting for. Waiting for a returning soldier? Waiting for a family reunion, gathering around grandparents, arms folding across, wishing longevity for the elders? Waiting to receive the red envelopes? Waiting for new set of clothes? Waiting for the sound of the first firecrackers, to step out to the altar in front of the house, lighting incense and offering prayers for the New Year? Waiting for a friendly card game with some friends? Or simply waiting for the carefree days, unburdened, riding a bike to visit teachers and classmates?

What's left to dream from the wings of Spring butterflies? What's left of the New Year's Eve night, folding paper money into butterfly shapes, hanging them on branches of golden apricot blossoms on the altar, behind the shiny bronze statues, next to the tray of fruits, beside the watermelon? Spring suddenly appeared here in the small hall under the church basement. Tết suddenly arrived here through a gathering with fellow countrymen, getting a taste of the Vietnamese language one longed for.

After much preparation, Tết had finally arrived in the church basement. The festive atmosphere was meticulously crafted with hanging ornaments - red balloons, blue balloons, and colorful paper strewn across the ceiling - all thoughtfully arranged by Father Swanson. He had enlisted the help of the community to decorate the room in celebration of Tết. Additionally, two themed panels brought in by Hiển adorned a green board placed at the end of the room.

Under Father Swanson's enthusiastic guidance, everyone joined in singing the song 'Kumbaya' to honor God. Though it was more of a collective hum, 'Kum-ba-ya... Kum-ba-ya...'

Following the heartwarming melody, Father Swanson joyfully assumed the role of elder, distributing lucky money envelopes to the young ones. Many lucky money envelopes were also sent to the children of local volunteers who had generously helped organize the first Tết celebration for the Vietnamese community.

Once the festivities concluded, Uncle Quý, an elder in the community, volunteered to lead the traditional Tết couplet game. Everyone praised his literary and meaningful verses, lively speech, and charming demeanor. The couplet he claimed to be timeless and unchallenged for decades was one from Thế Lữ, an exceptional poet and writer from the 1930s. Tuất, being young and not one to easily accept defeat, was eager to take on the challenge. He raised his hand to request permission to respond, on the spot, with another couplet of his own. While his response may not be equally immortal, it certainly made everyone in the room fall off their chairs laughing. All worries vanished, and everyone left the first overseas Tết celebration with joy. Some wrapped themselves in bulky jackets, some wore parkas, some wore high boots, some wore rubber sandals, confidently stepping into the indefinite night outside, facing the reality of minus 20 degrees Celsius, trekking through the snow for ten, fifteen, twenty minutes before reaching home. The new year had begun, and it must begin - for oneself, for one's children, and for the remaining family back in the homeland. Each left the celebration with their own feelings and thoughts.

8. Country never far away

In the middle of winter in Manitoba, outside is freezing cold. Today is Tuesday, and Tuất eagerly looks forward to the weekend. Last night, Alek called to inquire about Tuất, as he often does. But this time, he also invited Tuất for a weekend ice fishing trip. Tuất was surprised, 'What kind of fishing in the middle of winter?' The Filipino and Vietnamese fishing friends around here have set aside their fishing rods and are eagerly waiting for the next summer to come!

Tuất was born and raised amidst the rivers and waters of the Mekong Delta region, so he is no stranger to catching fish or trapping shrimp. However, when Alek repeatedly mentioned 'Ice Fishing,' Tuất felt very perplexed, unsure if Alek was actually inviting him to go fishing. Clearly, 'Fishing' means 'Câu cá' in Vietnamese, but 'Ice' is 'Nước đá.' Although Tuất's knowledge of the English language was not proficient, he believed he had not misheard these two English words, especially after asking multiple times to be sure. So, Tuất wondered if he should read the term backward, as he had learned in the refugee camp about English syntax. In this case, should the term 'ice fishing' be understood as 'fishing ice' instead?

Tuất didn't have to wait long for the answer. A week of busy work at the car repair shop quickly passed. On Saturday morning, precisely at the agreed time of 11 AM, Alek drove a pickup truck, carrying his fifteen-year-old son, to the front of the boarding house. Tuất walked up to the car, about to open the door, and noticed three fishing rods in the back of the truck. 'So, it's real fishing,' Tuất whispered to himself. As the car reached the highway, all around was blinding white snow, leaving only the black asphalt visible on the straight road ahead. On one side of the road was the vast expanse of smooth, shimmering white snow, covering what used to be cornfields. On the other side were the pine forests laden heavily with clumps of white snow on the branches. After a little over an hour, Alek slowed the car and turned right onto the road leading to Pine Lake.

Tuất had the opportunity to visit Pine Lake a few months ago on an outing with fellow refugees. The lake was about four hundred meters from the road, hidden behind the towering old pine trees, with dense bushes and tall trees reaching above one's head, intertwining and clinging to each other, providing shelter for the lake and enhancing its wild and tranquil beauty. At that time, it was late autumn, and apart from the everlasting green pines, the lower branches and leaves had turned yellow, purple, and even the wine-red of some blueberry bushes. A closer look revealed the faint dark spots of sweet berries that some mother bears and their cubs hadn't finished eating, still hanging on the branches. On the calm and smooth surface of the lake, a few yellow leaves floated, adding to the poetic scene. Suddenly, a gust of wind blew, detaching a few leaves, which drifted lazily on the lake's surface, reminding of the Autumn verses by the famous poet Nguyễn Khuyến, which Mr. Văn, the nineth-grade teacher, had made Tuất's group memorize:

'The autumn pond is cold, the water is clear,
A fishing boat is so tiny.
Azure waves ripple with the breeze,
A golden leaf swiftly carried by the wind.'

Although at Pine Lake, it lacks a small fishing boat, the gentle waves still follow the faint breeze, and it is quiet enough to hear the rustle of leaves somewhere.

- Here we are, we have arrived!

Alek's exclamation, with his familiar playful tone, brought Tuất back to reality. Young Alek adjusted the woolen toque on his golden, shimmering hair and cheerfully opened the car door. Tuất followed suit, looking around, finding no traces of water or the autumn waves on the lake's surface. However, relying on the position of the ancient pine trees on this side of the lake and the gentle hill rising on the opposite shore, Tuất could still envision the lake's location amidst the vast snowy fields. Everywhere one looked, there was only snow, pure, dazzling white snow.

Looking back, Tuất noticed that Alek and his father were unloading something from the truck, but it wasn't fishing rods. Upon closer inspection, Tuất figured it out. It was an ice auger. So, that's what 'Ice Fishing' is all about, Tuất thought. After a few weeks into winter, beneath the snow covering the surface, the lake had frozen, with ice nearly half a meter thick in some places. Yet, fish still thrived beneath. To fish, one needed only to drill a hole through the ice to drop the bait deep into the water, sometimes near the lake's bed. Then, they would gather, sit, and chat while waiting for a fish to bite.

Luckily, the ice wasn't too thick, so within no time, three fishing holes were drilled randomly across the lake. Alek courteously let Tuất choose his fishing rod first and patted Tuất on the back, encouraging a friendly competition to see who could catch more fish. Among the three fishing rods, there wasn't much difference; they were all like slender, small sticks. Compared to the thick bamboo fishing rods at Tuất's hometown, which were twice or thrice as long, these were merely 'toothpick' rods, Tuất chuckled at the thought. Seeing two rods in blue and one in red, Tuất picked the blue one, deliberately giving Alek and his father the choice between blue and red. As Tuất reaching for his chosen fishing rod, and before he could step back, Alek and his son enthusiastically jumped in to wrestle for the remaining blue fishing rod.

- I first!

- I first!

The father and son playfully tugged and pulled, each wanting to claim the blue fishing rod.

"If only I had known they liked the color blue this much, I would have left the blue rod for them," Tuất thought to himself. Eventually, Alek gave in to his son. Holding the red rod, Alek came over to explain to Tuất that his son really liked the bait on that blue rod. He believed that specific bait was lucky, helping him catch more fish. Tuất vaguely understood Alek's intent.

"So, they were competing for the bait, not the color of the fishing rods," Tuất thought. Being an avid fisherman, Tuất naturally understood that. Back in his hometown, what fisherman wouldn't know the importance of baits? You'd bait the hook according to the fish you were targeting: worms for catching catfish, mini frogs for snakehead fish, and moldy rice bait for gourami fish. Alternatively, you'd poke ant nests on guava trees to make the ants' eggs fall, then pick them up to use as bait. This would guarantee a delicious dish of fried gourami on the dinner table that day. Or at least a bowl of tasty melon soup with gourami.

Tuất looked down at the end of his fishing line to check if he had bait. It was strange; the bait was already attached, but it was artificial. It resembled a shiny piece of metal shaped like a minnow, with a sharp hook the size of a fingertip dangling at its tail. Tuất was flabbergasted: Canadian fish must all be blind to bite this kind of bait. Not only was the bait too artificial, but it also flaunted a sharp, gleaming hook in the middle of the pristine white setting.

In Tuất's village, people only used live bait. After hooking the bait, they would carefully add a blade of grass to the sharp end of the hook for camouflage. Even in the afternoons when they wanted to invite each other to go fishing by the ditch, they would speak in veiled terms among friends, never daring to openly say they were going fishing. They feared that the fish spirit would hear and warn all the fish to stay away.

Curious, Tuất glanced at the favorite bait of Alek's son. He was even more astonished. It was just a plastic tube, green like a leaf, with protruding frog-like eyes, painted white with two black dots in the middle, resembling a child's toy. But hanging at the tail, there wasn't just one, but three fierce-looking hooks, slanting towards three directions. Yet, the fish still took the bait. Unbelievable!

Tuất was still wondering when he saw Alek pull the folding chair out and sit by the edge of his fishing hole, beginning to drop the bait into the water down below and announcing the start of the fishing competition. Alek's son and Tuất quickly hurried to their respective fishing holes, grabbing the chair to sit and eagerly cast their fishing lines in full anticipation. Alek held the fishing rod, ready and waiting.

The atmosphere was tense. Alek gazed into the distance, a tranquil space with no trace of other souls disturbing the pristine snow-covered surface. Alek tilted his face upwards, turning towards the sun as if trying to fully absorb each warm sunbeam from its source, from the celestial bodies. He joyfully exclaimed:

- Excellent, there's nothing better.

At the same time, Alek's son cheered:

- I got one, I got one!

Indeed, that kid was quite a skilled angler, Tuất thought to himself. He had caught a Northern Pike, a fish native to the cold waters of the north. The fish's meat was delicious, but its appearance was ancient-like with a rugged, flattened head reminiscent of a crocodile. Its body was tube-shaped and elongated, olive green with scattered yellowish spots, not unlike a spotted moray eel.

This species of fish was very aggressive. Alek had been intimidated by it once. During a summer fishing trip a few years ago, Alek recalled, he was standing on a rock by the riverbank, absentmindedly gazing at the sky and clouds, performing a repetitive motion - casting the bait far into the river and then reeling it in. Casting out... reeling in.... Then, one time, after reeling the bait close to his feet, Alek suddenly encountered a Northern Pike leaping out of the water, chasing the bait in mid-air, just inches away from him. He was so startled, thinking he was under attack by the fish.

Alek opened his tackle box, grabbed a long-handled pair of pliers to help his child remove the hook from the fish's mouth, which had sharp, protruding teeth. After both father and son marveled at their catch, Alek released the fish back into the lake, much to Tuất's surprise. Alek and his son didn't fish for food; they saw fishing as a recreational sport. Tuất was amazed, witnessing such a game for the first time. He watched the fish swim away with a pang of regret, 'That fish, if grilled, would have been so delicious.

After a few minutes of excitement and restlessness, Alek's child began to feel hungry and called out for food. Everyone pulled their seats and gathered by Alek's fishing pit to have lunch. Alek handed each person a small paper plate with three slices of cheese, a few celery sticks, and a couple of baby carrots the size of a pinky finger. A few minutes later, he pulled a carton of fresh milk and a bottle of red wine with two plastic cups from his backpack for his child and himself. He turned to Tuất and squinted, saying, 'We need this to keep our bodies warm, not to mention it goes well with the cheese.'

Tuất looked at the food on the plate, thinking to himself, 'Well, people do what they do, but what a hardship in eating!' Once again, Tuất felt regret for missing the chance to have grilled fish for a meal, or at least a fish stew or something. Alek and his child reminisced about the suspenseful and thrilling moments in the hockey game on TV last night. It was an ice game, with two teams each using sticks to hit a heavy round disc into the opposing team's goal. The disc was black and just about the size of an adult's palm, making it hard to follow on TV. Tuất couldn't understand how it could become a game with such national fervor and spirit in this country.

Looking down at the plate, Tuất noticed an old celery stick that he had intended to discard. He absentmindedly picked it up and put it in his mouth. Crunchy. Absentmindedly gazing at the high sky, a scattered cloud was drifting in from some distant place. Really far away. Echoes of childhood lingered in Tuất's ears:

- Grandma, look. I've finished all the rice in the bowl. Not wasting a single grain.

- Yes, my grandson. You are really good!

Meanwhile, Alek and his son had shifted their topic without Tuất realizing. They engrossed in recalling memories from the deer hunting trip in the nearby forest a few months ago.

9. Memories of a River

Lately, whenever I have the opportunity to see images of the bustling cities in Vietnam nowadays, I can't help but notice the absence of the familiar 'áo dài' robes, the traditional long tunic worn by Vietnamese women, that once graced our beloved streets. It brings back memories of a river.

So here's the thing. Although I was born and raised in an area surrounded by rivers and streams, swimming never came naturally to me, not like fish to water, or smoothly like a ferry crossing a river. It all started at the bank of the river near my house, when my mother enrolled me in swimming lessons with Mr. Sáu. He was well past sixty, with few teeth left, but his skin was weathered like bronze. His voice, though somewhat hoarse from years of drinking potent liquor, carried great strength. Thanks to his robust lungs, many believed that. At every swimming class opening ceremony, he would perform a breathtaking dive for parents and students alike to watch from the shore of the river. No one kept track of how long he stayed submerged. All that was known was that from the moment he disappeared beneath the surface until worried murmurs arose from the crowd on the shore, it had been quite a while. Yet the villagers had to hold their breath for another couple of moments before suddenly witnessing him emerge in the middle of the river. The villagers were thoroughly impressed and felt reassured entrusting their children to him for swimming lessons.

Not only was he skilled, but he also practiced his profession with great professionalism and formality. On the first day of swimming lessons with him, before entering the water, students had to perform a proper "initiation" ceremony. They had to pay respects to their ancestors, and make offerings to the departed spirits in front of an altar set with offerings of food, incense, and wine, laid out on the grass by the riverbank. After the ceremony, he scattered rice and salt along the riverbank before allowing the students to divide the offerings among themselves to eat. Mr. Sáu never forgot to take a sip of rice wine to warm his stomach before getting into the water.

After a few hesitant days, a group of boys, disciples of Mr. Sáu, began to feel comfortable in the water, playing like unruly ones, from above the bank down to inside the water. Poor Mr. Sáu had to keep bustling about, teaching one while keeping an eye on the others. But all good times come to an end. After a few weeks of the boys' enjoyment, one day he introduced a new student, my neighbor. Seriously, she was a troublemaker! At school, girls and boys studied separately, so why was she here? Some boys and I wondered. Who would learn to swim with a girl?

Girls are strange. They brought a broom to school to sweep the classroom. In the afternoon, they even carried the teacher's bag for her. Sometimes they would even take the tablecloth from the teacher's desk home to wash. My days of swimming lessons have become a nightmare since then. Don't wrongly accuse me; there must be another hidden reason to explain my suffering and that of the boys. Our feelings at that time towards the neighbor girl have nothing to do with the fact that she had previously taken swimming lessons, and Mr. Sáu often called her out to "perform" her swimming style for the boys! I've hated swimming in the river ever since.

Fortunately, time is indeed a precious remedy, as our grandparents used to say. Although her house is close to mine, I had never paid attention to her before the swimming lessons. Even after a few weeks of swimming lessons, I didn't pay much attention. It's just that, in the following days and months, every morning I enjoyed standing by the fence, admiring the scene of the street in front of the house waking up in the morning sun. The hustle and bustle of people passing by, some carrying baskets to the market, others riding bikes to work, and students carrying their bags to school. If by chance among them was the neighbor girl tagging along with her mother to the market, smiling shyly at me, then at most I just felt like the sun was rising for the second time that day. All the resentment I had towards the river, following that trend, dissipated like thin mist in the morning sun, leaving behind a longing for the river. Reminiscing of the ragged shirt of a little girl, fluttering with each playful step on the riverbank during our swimming lessons, now replaced by a neatly well-pressed 'áo bà ba', a traditional short garment for women, thinly fitted to the slender girl who snugly tucked beside her mother.

Perhaps that's why not long after, I found myself enjoying "river bathing" again. In the late afternoon, waiting for the water to rise, taking a stroll to the river for a "bath" had become a small joy that I looked forward to all day. When I say "river bathing," it's actually swimming, playing in the water with the neighborhood kids. I became addicted to river bathing perhaps because I missed the coconut leave stems or the banana trunks that we used to fight over to hold onto as floats, even though we didn't need floats anymore. It could also be because I missed the game of catching shrimp and prawns (holding hands underwater, quickly squeezing to release water between the thumb and index finger, if water spurts up high, it's a shrimp, otherwise, it's a prawn), or simply because I loved the flow of the river. I loved diving underwater, letting the river water caress my hair, face, and body, soaking every cell, cooling the skin and flesh. After resurfacing, with water still lingering on my hair, streaming down my face, I had to quickly wipe it away to catch my first breath again in the ultimate refreshing feeling.

Some day, feeling adventurous, a few of us kids decided to swim from this side of the river to the other to play. However, because it was a wide stretch of river, we often had to wait for a ferry to take people across before swimming to make sure it was safe. If someone got exhausted or stumbled midway, they could cling to the ferry or someone would notice and rescue them. On the way from my house to the riverbank, I naturally had to pass by my neighbor's house. But that had nothing to do with my love for river bathing. Because on those rare occasions when I happened to see her sitting in front of her house, she would give me a friendly glance, a cheerful smile, and on those days, I might feel a bit more enthusiastic, a bit more foolish, just enough to forget about caution and swim across the large river without waiting for the ferry. Oh, the power of... the river!

Through many moons of water flowing under the bridge and stepping into high school, the image of the 'bà ba' garment gradually gave way to the distinctive features of the flowing white dress (áo dài), draped over a swaying figure, always fluttering in the wind and trailing gracefully behind. I could recognize it from afar, very far away, from the bridge at the end of the road leading to our houses. Every time, by chance, I sat on the railing in front of my house and encountered the 'long dress' (áo dài) returning from school, offering me a welcoming smile, it was enough to make my heart sing. But strangely enough, sometimes the heart seems to know beforehand, so it would sing joyfully before my eyes caught sight of that long dress.

But every river eventually has its bends. Not long after, on a leisurely afternoon, standing by the house's porch, under the cool shade of the guava tree, I was about to reach for a delicious guava on a lower branch, to pick it for a bite to ease my craving. Suddenly, a strange feeling made me look out to the street in front of the house. I was startled. It turned out to be the neighbor girl, dressed up in her first Western lady dress. A long white dress with little red flowers reaching her knees.

A sense of loss consumed me as I stood there, overwhelmed by emotions. A lump formed in my throat, and I felt the sting of tears welling up in the corners of my eyes. I couldn't help but cry - for the departure without a proper farewell of the familiar long white Vietnamese tunic. It wasn't just because, in that moment, I glanced back at my own bare body, clad only in a pair of worn-out black shorts, feeling akin to a destitute coal seller pining for a princess in some beloved classic tale. Thankfully, the guava in my hand remained unripe, still firm; otherwise, it might have met the same fate as the orange in Trần Quốc Toản's grip. Legend has it that he crushed an orange in his bare hand in a fit of rage upon hearing news of the enemy's invasion of his homeland.

Since then, every afternoon, the people in the neighborhood no longer catch sight of me leisurely strolling along the riverbank. Instead, I find myself engrossed in crafting melancholic poetry.

*"Sister, I've known you since the days of river baths,
When you ran barefoot, clad in your 'bà ba' shirt."*

Hmm, not quite there yet, still a tad too simplistic.

*"As the tides ebb and flow, lost in their own rhythm,
You've already dreamt of the elegant 'áo dài' after a few moons."*

Too idealistic!

*"As surprised to witness the river drying up,
Confused by the sight of someone donning Western attire."*

Too somber!

*"The water flows, carrying away the 'bà ba' shirt,
And with it, the flowing tails of my sister's áo dài."*

More simple and heartfelt, but it may be a tat confusing. Perhaps the root of the issue lies with my mother, who taught me to address female peers as 'Sister'!

Roughly speaking, I've traversed from beginning to end the corridors of memory, exploring why the absence of the 'áo dài' silhouette on the bustling streets of Vietnam today resonates with the ebb and flow of a river. Yet, beneath this observation lies a persistent inquiry: what sparked the vanishing of the 'áo dài'? Could it be that the push towards a more abbreviated or Westernized attire for women was deemed necessary for their liberation within an evolving industrial society? Certainly, practical considerations arise, such as the compatibility of the traditional 'áo dài' with the demands of modern industrial workplaces. But must we forsake its entire cultural significance?

Much like the ritual offering of fruits to the river spirits by Mr. Sáu, the venerable swim instructor, considered by some as a superstitious practice, the 'áo dài' may have been deemed by some as an outdated form in need of replacement. Nevertheless, Mr. Sáu's ritual could serve as a reminder of the mentor's role and the solemn responsibility it entails, imbuing students with a sense of gravity in their pursuits, despite the inevitable allure of youthful exuberance. Similarly, the graceful allure of the 'áo dài', transcending its mere aesthetic, has evolved into a beacon of exemplary etiquette for Vietnamese women. As the world bestows upon it the mantle of a cherished heritage of humanity, shouldn't it, then, command even greater reverence and preservation? Cherishing the elegance of the 'Áo dài' and honoring its legacy thus allow its threads to weave the fabric of collective identity, not just for the daughters, but also for the sons of the legendary Mother Âu Cơ.

Notes

1. Poem: 'Đoạn Trường Tân Thanh' (The Tale of Kiều); Author: Nguyễn Du.
2. Song: 'Kỷ Vật Cho Em'; Songwriter: Phạm Duy.
3. Play: 'Người Vợ Không Bao Giờ Cưới'; Playwright: Kiên Giang.
4. Play: 'Tình Anh Bán Chiếu'; Playwright: Viễn Châu.
5. Song: 'Trường Ca Con Đường Cái Quan'; Songwriter: Phạm Duy. Song: 'Một Chuyến Bay Đêm'; Songwriters: Song Ngọc & Hoài Linh.
6. Ban Kích Động Nhạc AVT từ 1966 trở về sau gồm có các ca nhạc sĩ Lữ Liên (thay vì Anh Linh lúc bắt đầu thành lập), Vân Sơn và Tuấn Đăng.
7. Song: 'Bạch Đằng Giang'; Songwriters: Lưu Hữu Phước and Nguyễn Thành Nguyên.
8. Song: 'Khỏe Vì Nước'; Songwriter: Hùng Lân.
9. Song: 'Hè Về'; Songwriter: Hùng Lân.
10. Song: 'Nỗi Buồn Hoa Phượng'; Songwriter: Thanh Sơn.
11. Song: 'Ly Rượu Mừng'; Songwriter: Phạm Đình Chương.
12. Song: 'Ngày Hạnh Phúc'; Songwriter: Lam Phương.
13. 'Ngụ Ngôn Mùa Đông'; Nhạc sĩ Trịnh Công Sơn.
14. Poem: 'Chinh Phụ Ngâm Khúc'; Author: Đặng Trần Côn; 'Nôm' script by: Đoàn Thị Điểm.

Author

Vinh Quyen Tang
(Tăng Quyền Vinh)
Ottawa, Canada.

Books published:

1. Bên Kia Bến Đỗ, 2021.
2. Đứa Con An Giang, 2022.
3. Lu nước ngọt, 2023.
4. Nails Tình Thương, 2023.
5. The Boy From An Giang: A Journey Through AI-Assisted Translation, 2023 (Under revision).
6. Tứ Quý (Truyện trích từ Bên Kia Bến Đỗ), 2023.
7. The Precious Quartet (Selected Tales from Bên Kia Bến Đỗ), 2024.
8. Compassionate Nails: A Journey of Love and Resilience (Translated from the Vietnamese title 'Nails Tình Thương'), 2024.
9. Đôi Dòng Sông Nước, 2024
10. Tales of the River: Journey from the Mekong Delta, 2024.

ISBN 978-1-7381921-8-2